MW01138236

FIEND

CRAVINGS #2

RACHAEL
ORMAN

Cover:
Night Vulture Products
Shay Iverson

Cover Design:
Phycel Designs

Editing:
Editing Juggernaut

Fiend

Acknowledgements

As always, I owe *everything* to my one and only sweetie.

Jacqui – You crazy Aussie.. I love you lady!

Editing Juggernaut – Thank you for being so AWESOME and always working with me even with crazy deadlines!

Phycel Designs – Once again…. Perfection.

Shay – It was wonderful getting to know you and I couldn't be happier with having you grace the cover of one of my books.

And every other single reader out there – without you, I wouldn't be doing what I love to do so thank you for your continued support.

fiend

noun \\'fēnd\\

: an evil spirit : a demon or devil
: a very evil or cruel person
: a person who is very enthusiastic about something

Chapter 1

Alix

Finally being able to see Master and knowing he was John, the man I'd lusted after for so long, made me so incredibly hot. I needed him in ways I had never needed another person.

Standing naked in front of him, clad only in a pair of dress slacks, made my pussy clench as my tongue darted out to wet my lips. The beauty of his hard muscles made me shiver in anticipation. While I'd been allowed to run my hands along his body before, it was different when I could see him and his reactions while doing it. From the hard bulge under my hand, it wasn't hard to tell he was just as aroused as I was.

A smile tugged at the corner of his mouth as I finally released his straining cock from his pants. As soon as my hand wrapped around the swollen flesh, his fingers gripped my wrist.

"No, Precious." Two simple words. That was all it took for him to put me in my place and remind me he was the one in charge, even if I was dying to get my hands on him.

Lowering my head, I took on the submissive form I knew most men expected. While I wasn't experienced in the scene, I had done a lot of research since John had started revealing all the wonderful things I came to love and need from my Master.

"Look at me," he said in a deep, commanding voice that made my eyes snap up to his blue ones, which glowed in the dim lighting. "When it is just us, I want your eyes on me at *all* times. I don't want you looking down. I don't want to see the top of your head. I want to see every drop of pleasure you are experiencing as it flashes across your eyes."

"Yes, Master." I fought the urge to drop my head again. Being able to look into his eyes was something I'd have to get used to. The blindfold I'd once worn had trained me to keep my eyes closed or down when I was with him since I couldn't see anyway.

"Get on the bed," John instructed as he stepped out of his pants, which had pooled around his feet, and then his shoes and socks.

I stepped backwards until I encountered the bed and sat on the edge.

"Lie back on the center." Placing his hands on his hips, he waited for me to do as I was told before approaching slowly. "Beautiful. Absolutely stunning," he murmured, his eyes caressing my exposed body as he took in all of me.

Feeling my cheeks burn at the compliment, I forced a smile. No one had ever looked at me with the appreciation — the *hunger* — I saw in his eyes. I didn't know how to react to the man I'd wanted for so long peering at me with such desire. Normally, I was uncomfortable with my body, but his expression made it hard to remember why.

John moved to stand at the foot of the bed as he continued to devour me with his eyes. Reaching out, his large hands grabbed my ankles before roughly parting them. "Fuck." A low, deep growl filled the quiet space. Reaching to the side of the mattress, he pulled nylon restraints from one side, then the other, before carefully tying my ankles so I couldn't close my legs. "I hope you understand that by showing up here tonight — You. Are. Mine. There is no going back. I am going to claim every part of you. Every single inch of your body will know who it belongs to when we're done."

Hearing his roughened voice as the heat of his breath rushed down my spread thighs, my breath caught and my hands dug into the bedding beneath me. I wanted to touch him, I wanted him to touch me. Instead, I would wait until my master deemed it the right time. It was the reason I had returned to him. I needed what he could give me. In more ways than one.

Running his hands up my legs, he stopped when he got to my inner thighs. All my nerves were focused on the points where his fingers momentarily dug into the sensitive skin. Moving to kneel between my spread thighs, his hands

3

moved up to my hips, once again digging in as he gripped them hard. His eyes constantly drank in my body, making my insecurities flare up. Then his eyes lifted to mine and everything but him simply vanished.

"I want to do so much to you, but all I can think about is finally getting my dick inside you," John said, licking his lips.

"I'm yours, Master." I spoke softly and raised my arms above my head, showing him that even though my arms weren't restrained, I wasn't going to stop him. He wouldn't hurt me, not in a way I wouldn't enjoy.

"You are so damn perfect." John slid his hands up my stomach, then between my breasts, until he could cup either side of my neck. Roughly, he pulled me into a sitting position as he lowered his head. Our lips joined in a rough kiss, teeth bumping before they spread and our tongues met. Pulling back, he continued to hold my neck as he looked directly into my eyes. "Tell me you are on the pill."

"I am," I whispered. As soon as the words were out of my lips, his cock was sliding through the moisture pooling between my thighs. Once lined up, he thrust deep in one hard push.

My head fell as far backwards as it could with his hands still holding me up as a shriek leapt unbidden from my throat. I pressed my hands into the bed to help support my weight. Looking down, I could watch as he plunged in and out of my body. His cock was beautiful, slicked and hard. The sight made my orgasm grow closer. "John. Master. Oh. My. God."

"Come, Precious. Come for me while you watch me fuck you." His voice was gravelly and his grip on my nape tightened as he continued the hard, fast rhythm.

Finally, my release eased and thankfully, he lowered me back onto the bed. I didn't think he could possibly get any deeper, but he shifted my hips, changing the angle he entered me at. I couldn't help but grunt with each plunge as he hit my cervix — he was going so deep. It hurt, but in a new, unexpected way and there wasn't a chance in hell I would tell him to stop. The rivulets of sweat running down his muscular chest, along with his muscles rippling and flexing with each movement, showed how hard he was working. It made my mouth water to get a taste of him, his sweat.

Surprisingly, he kept at it for longer than I thought he would be able to and my body started to stir to life again. Gripping the sheets in my fists, I arched my back, helping him get deeper. I pushed off the bed so I could rise up onto my elbows, then sank a hand into his hair. Pulling his mouth to mine, I dropped back to the bed, making him follow me down. It was amazing having John's body pressed so firmly to mine as he continued to thrust, slowing due to the new position. Releasing his mouth, but not his hair, I looked into his eyes. "You feel so good, Master."

"Shit." John clenched his jaw as his entire body hardened. A few grunts and erratic thrusts let me know he'd finally found his own release. Each thigh flopped to either side as his weight pressed into me.

"You make me lose control," he murmured softly into my ear.

"Good." I smiled as my hand drifted lazily down his sweat-covered back. "I was beginning to think you could go all night."

"Oh, Precious, we aren't done. I just need a breather." He pulled back and smiled down at me before slowly stepping back. Dropping to his knees between my thighs, his fingers plunged unexpectedly into me.

Rising onto my hands, I looked down at him in confusion. Surely he didn't expect to start back up so soon.

"I'm making sure my seed doesn't escape. I told you, you are mine, and I want a part of me inside you as long as possible. Don't move," He demanded, back in full Dom mode. Stepping away from the bed, he grabbed something from the small dresser before returning. A large, cold object pressed against my opening. "You will wear this until the next time I fill you."

The object slid into my body and then John fiddled with straps of some sort. When I realized what he was doing, I tried to pull back. "What are you doing? I can't wear this."

"What was that, Precious?" John cocked his head, his eyes blazing with anger.

"Wh...What is it?" I tried a different approach.

"It's a dildo... and a harness that'll lock it in place," John said as if it were normal. I felt like it was anything but.

"But..." I blinked rapidly, trying to comprehend what he was saying.

"Don't worry, Alix. I plan on fucking you again very soon, so you won't have to wear it for long. This time." John rubbed a thumb over my cheek before giving me a tender kiss. "I can't help it. I have to claim you."

Fighting my need to please him and the uncomfortable feeling of having an object that was going to be staying in my body, I closed my eyes and took a deep breath. I trusted John. He was my Dom. Finally, I swallowed hard before nodding and opening my eyes to look at him. "Whatever you'd like, Master."

"Fuck, that's hot." John's hand sank into my hair as he pulled me to him for a heated kiss. Sliding his tongue along mine, he groaned into my mouth. "I love having you without the blindfold."

"I love not having the blindfold." I smiled. While I'd been shocked the man I'd been calling my master was also the man I frequently masturbated to, it was almost a dream. I wanted him. He wanted me. That's what was important. The fact we both apparently had the same kinks made everything so much better. We clicked in ways you couldn't fabricate. They were simply there or they weren't.

"Now, Precious, I think we have a punishment to take care of, yes?" John reached to either side to release my ankles from the restraints.

"I'm sorry, sir. I don't know what you are referring to." And I didn't. The last day had been a blur more than anything since I unexpectedly discovered his identity.

"Let's see." Holding out a hand, he helped me to my feet before spinning me around and pressing against my back. "It was in your office." A cool band enclosed my throat. *The collar.* "And you were being naughty. Does that help clear things up?"

I ducked my head — it *did* clear things up. He had caught me masturbating when I'd been explicitly told not to. He'd told me that he had a special punishment in mind for when I gave in to my addiction. I didn't want to find out what it was, but I had indeed touched myself. It had been more out of a desire to upset him than the need for release it had once been. I doubted it would matter to him, though.

"Come," John said as I felt the telltale tug from the front of my throat. *The leash.*

Clenching my jaw, I turned to follow him. To my surprise, he had pulled on a pair of black boxers, but left me completely nude. He led me out of the room without another word.

Although we had been into the big room where lots of couples played at once, it was completely different heading that way without a blindfold and with a dildo keeping his come inside me. My palms grew more damp with each step.

With only a few feet left in the hallway, John turned to me. He tugged my leash at the same time he stepped closer, making me bump against his bare chest.

"Breathe," he whispered as a hand cupped my cheek. "There is no judging here. It is a community of like-minded individuals. No one will touch you except me. You ready?"

"Yes, sir." I didn't know if I really was, but I was going to do it because he would be the one leading me.

After dragging his thumb across my lower lip, he turned to enter the room.

Chapter 2

John

Finally getting inside Alix had been as fantastic as I'd dreamed about, but the absolute best part had been filling her with my release and then plugging her up. It was me that was in her. My come that filled the most intimate part of her, and it stayed there. I told her I would fuck her again, but I didn't specify where.

I wanted to show her what her punishment was going to be. It wouldn't be right away, but I would make her endure it when she was least expecting it. She would, however, get to watch as another experienced it so she could anticipate what it would be like. Anticipation always made it that much more fun for everyone involved.

Slightly tugging on the leash, I led her into the main room of Scene, the BDSM club where I kept the private room we had been in. I knew she was anxious, as it was the first time she would be there with me and without a blindfold, but she had seen it the first time she'd come with her friend. She would not be the only nude person in the room — part of the joy of being in an environment of like-minded people. It wasn't unusual, it wasn't weird or awkward. It was simply another person who enjoyed kink.

Without stopping or acknowledging anyone along the way, I walked straight to the back. It was a room that had been shut off during her first visit, so I paused and turned to look at her. While I wanted to shock her, I didn't want it to be overwhelming. Her punishment had to be something she feared and didn't want to ever suffer again, as it would be the only thing that would help her not give into her addiction again.

I knew she had most likely been attempting to get my attention, and she had certainly done that, but not in a good way. I'd given her rules for a reason and no matter her rationale for breaking them, a punishment would be given.

Cradling her cheek, I lowered my chin so I was looking directly into her eyes. "Watch closely, Precious. This is what your punishment will be. Not now. No, I want you to think about how she feels, wonder when I will make you get up there. Will it be later tonight? Will it be next week? Is it only going to be for ten minutes or an hour?" I stepped closer, putting my mouth to her ear. "What's it going to feel like being forced to have orgasm after orgasm and being absolutely helpless to stop it? Maybe I'll invite a crowd in to watch. Or will it be just you and me? Think about it, because it is going to happen. You owe it to me."

"Yes, sir." Alix lifted her chin showing me she wasn't going to back down, but would accept her punishment even though she wasn't entirely sure what it was.

"Good girl." I patted her bare ass before stepping back to lead her to the far side of the room. "Kneel facing the center of the room. Watch everything that goes on there."

Without a word, she settled onto her knees, legs spread wide, palms down. It didn't take long before more spectators filed in, along with a shirtless man with his nude submissive. She had a leather mask over her face with holes for her to breathe through and a fuzzy tail swaying behind her with each step she took.

The sub was helped onto a bench before having her ankles and wrists bound so she was spread-eagled. Her Dom wheeled over the contraption I had brought Alix to see. An automatic vibrator. It was a machine that would thrust and withdraw at any speed it was set to while another part was lowered onto the clit if it was a female submissive to ensure endless stimulation.

Imagining Alix on the bench coming over and over had my cock elongating with excitement. She was absolutely the sexiest woman I'd ever laid eyes on, especially when she shared such new experiences with me. She'd abused her own body with pleasure, but she'd been a good girl for me, obeying all the rules I set upon her. It made her punishment for the single time she'd truly disobeyed me so much more impactful, to ensure she didn't get into the habit of doing it. While I enjoyed the power exchange we had, I didn't like punishing her. I didn't get off on making her hurt like that. It was so much better when she enjoyed what I was giving her as much as I was.

A soft whimper made me look at Alix. She was gnawing at her bottom lip, eyes focused on the scene taking place. I'd seen it numerous times and was excited more by the thought of hearing Alix come than anything else.

"What's wrong, Precious?" I asked.

Slowly she broke her line of sight and looked up at me. "Nothing, sir. Just watching as you instructed me to."

"Does it excite you? Is that why you're trembling?" From the way she was having a hard time keeping her legs spread, I could tell she was wet and needy.

"Yes, sir," she said after a moment.

"You can't wait to get your punishment?"

"No, sir. Not exactly."

"Then explain." I twisted the chain attached to her collar.

"It's the sounds she is making, sir." Alix sucked her bottom lip into her mouth again.

"Ah. See, I get hard imagining it is you up there making those noises." I dragged my tongue over my lower lip. Seeing how turned on she was, I didn't want to wait. "I want you to suck me off. Right here."

Her eyes grew wide, but she didn't hesitate to scoot over so she was in front of me. Using the easy-access pocket in the front of my boxer briefs, she withdrew my hard cock. Encasing it with one hand, she took the head in her mouth, swirling her tongue around it.

Sinking my hand into her hair, I fisted the strands tightly. Her mouth was hot and slick and nearly made my eyes cross.

More women than I'd admit to had gone down on me. It was less complicated than fucking them, but none of them even came close to having Alix on her knees in front of me. Maybe it was her skill, or maybe it was simply the fact that it was her which made it so much more erotic and feel so much better.

Tensing my thighs, I prepared myself for when she took me all the way into her mouth, letting my cock hit the back of her tight throat. As if knowing what I wanted, Alix sucked me deep. A groan was out of my throat before I could even think to stop it.

Alix used one hand to gently massage my balls while the other chased her mouth up and down my shaft.

"Damn, Alix," I exhaled when her hand on my balls slipped back to press against my perineum in time with her strokes.

She moaned when her lips were around the base, sending vibrations all the way through my dick.

I wasn't going to come, no matter how good she gave head. I had other plans for that and even if I didn't want to admit it, me and my dick weren't in our teens anymore. Getting off more than twice in a night was rare. Pulling on her hair that was still wrapped around my fist, she only moaned and fought me to keep sucking.

"Enough," I grunted harshly.

Frowning, she finally released my cock from her mouth and sat back on her knees. Her eyes were on the floor, but her pout was easy to see.

"Stop pouting," I said as I shoved my dick back into my briefs. "Have you seen enough to know what your punishment will be? And I won't be distracted when it's time for it by a little dick sucking."

"Yes, sir," she said, keeping her head down.

"Then let's get out of here." I tugged on her leash and she stood to follow me.

Once back in our room, I took the collar off her and threw it on the bed. Pushing her hair over her shoulders so it draped down her back, I traced her jawline with my fingertips before dropping them to her neck to flow over her shoulders. Finally, my hands found hers and I clasped them.

"I want to meet you outside of here. Go on a real date. Do things that don't involve sex," I said.

Her eyes lifted to meet mine for the first time since we'd entered the room. "Seriously?"

The question sent a red hot flare through my stomach. Was she going to refuse me after everything?

"Seriously." I swallowed and fought to keep my nerves from showing. I might be her dominant, but she could easily show me the door or only want to be with me while at the club.

"Of course. I didn't think *you* would want that." A smile spread over her face, lighting up her eyes. "I would love to."

Unable to hold back, I planted a soft kiss upon her lips. "I can't wait," I said, letting my lips brush against hers. Pulling back, I let go of her hands. Dropping my voice, I said, "Get on the bed."

From the stiffening of her spine and the way she rapidly moved to follow orders, I knew she understood I was once more her Dom. Climbing on the bed, she lay on her back, knees spread, obviously trying to entice me.

"Is this your way of telling me I haven't given your pussy enough attention?" I stepped closer to the bed while chastising her wantonness.

As the meaning of my words sank in, she closed her legs, lowering them on the bed so her feet nearly touched the footboard. "No, sir."

"Don't forget who's in charge here." I shoved off my briefs, then knelt next to her on the bed. "I have something special planned. See, I told you our first time together would be memorable and it isn't over yet."

"I can't wait to see what else you have in mind, sir." Alix bit her bottom lip as she quivered with excitement.

"Roll over," I instructed. When her beautiful round bottom came into view, my palm slapped it hard. Watching the bright red blossom over her cheek, I had to resist the urge to add a matching mark to the other side. Alix's soft moan didn't help my resolve. Grabbing both her hips in my hands, I lifted her so her knees supported her weight, making her ass stick in the air. The harness was working perfectly, keeping the dildo firmly in place. Pushing against it caused Alix to gasp. "Oh, forget that was there, Precious?"

"N... no, sir. Just didn't expect... the movement," she said, her voice muffled from the bed.

Smiling, I reached around her to grab the bottle of lube from the small nightstand. A few drops was all I needed before dropping the bottle on the bed. With one hand I rubbed the lube over my erect cock while pulling and pushing on the harnessed dildo, mimicking thrusting. Once the lube was warmed and my cock was well-lubricated, I moved my hand between her cheeks. Rubbing two fingers against her puckered entrance, I slipped my other hand between her thighs to find her clit.

Even though from what I remembered she'd said she had never tried anal, she didn't jump or pull away at all as one of my fingers pushed into her back channel. Only going to my second knuckle, I pulled back to rub around the rim a few more times, keeping the rotations in time with my fingers on her clit. The next time I used two fingers to enter her, earning me a sigh of contentment and her ass pushing backwards, welcoming me.

Thrusting delicately, I eventually managed to get them all the way in, preparing her to take me. After giving her a few deep thrusts, I removed my fingers, causing her to whimper in protest, which made me slap her other cheek in warning.

My little subbie needed to learn to take what she was given without begging for more.

Grabbing hold of my cock, I trailed the head of it up and down her crack before lining it up with the slippery rosette. Even though I had prepped her, it would still be a battle to get in her tight hole and uncomfortable for her. One hand dipped around her leg to return to teasing her clit as my other one planted firmly on the top of her ass. Slowly, I pushed forward until her body opened up, welcoming me into its warmth.

"Oh," Alix gasped, and a shiver worked its way down her back. Still she didn't move, but I could see her hands fisted into the bed sheets.

Pulling out gently, I thrust back in, slightly deeper. Little by little, I sank my dick into her ass while teasing her clit the whole time. By the time my hips pressed against her beautiful bottom, she was moaning while rocking back and forth on her knees.

"Sir. Please. I need to come," Alix cried as she turned her head to try to look at me.

"Not yet, you don't," I snarled, releasing her clit from its torture. Digging both hands into her hips, I pulled back and let loose on her. I'd been as patient and caring as I could. The beast demanded to be let free and I let him take over, pounding into her ass relentlessly.

With each thrust, the harness shoved the dildo in and out. Alix was getting well and truly fucked. The first time with her had been nice, but that wasn't what I had been talking about when I told her she'd never forget our first time. Me taking her ass while my seed was still being shoved deep in her pussy. *That* was what I had been talking about. Making sure she was marked in every way possible. She was mine. Even little bits of my come were down her throat from her sucking my dick so well. I would make sure to fill her throat with my seed soon to make sure she remembered whose cock owned her body.

All I had left was to learn every part of her beautiful mind and make it mine as well. I had already started working on that.

"Master. Please," Alix whined.

Since I could feel my own release growing near, I growled, "Come, Precious."

The shriek that left her made my balls tighten with pride and my own orgasm washed over me as I spilled inside her. Once I could feel my legs again, I sadly pulled my dick from her before quickly undoing the harness straps and easing the dildo from her pussy.

Alix's knees slid out from under her and she lay still for a few moments before slowly rolling over to gaze at me. "Amazing." Her eyelids slowly closed before opening again.

"I need to go, but there is one thing I would like to do first," I said, pulling on my briefs again.

"What's that?" Alix breathed, taking longer to open her eyes.

I retrieved an item from my trouser pocket before dropping them back to the ground again. Returning to the bed, I sat next to her. "Something I've been wanting to return to you."

I held up a hand, letting the strand of pearls drop from my fingers to swing between us.

"More pearls." Alix smiled.

"No. These are your pearls. The first strand. Your collar. The ones you are never to take off. The other ones can be added or taken off whenever you'd like, but these are to always stay on unless I take them off or you decide you no longer want to be my submissive." Using both hands, I clasped the necklace around her neck before pulling her hair out from it. "They look beautiful. You make them beautiful."

"Thank you, Master," Alix exhaled as she trailed her fingers along the strand.

Chapter 3

Alix

After Master gave me back my necklace, he redressed before leaving me on the bed with a soft kiss to my forehead. I was worn out. Never before had I been so thoroughly fucked or so incredibly relaxed. There was a peacefulness surrounding me that made me never want to move.

Eventually I managed to make myself get out of the bed and go home. I didn't want to, but it wasn't as much fun to be in our playroom when Master wasn't there. Not to mention it had to be the middle of the night or extremely early morning hours. At least I didn't have to work tomorrow so I could spend all day at home in my bed.

Except by the time I pulled into my driveway, I realized I had multiple texts that I would have to answer before crashing. Most of them were from Jennifer, who apparently had a lot to say. The last one was from Master. I responded to his first. He'd simply asked me to let him know when I got home.

I am now home. Thank you for my necklace back. I missed it. I can't wait for our date.

Falling back onto the couch, I opened the string of messages from Jennifer. She was rambling on and on about her night and how crazy it was and how she'd happened to run into this guy she'd hooked up with in the past. After many long messages, I made it to the most recent one.

I'm glad you found the man who knocked your socks off again. Long night here. Just getting to bed. Talk to you later.

Yawning, I tried to find the energy to make it to my bedroom. Instead, I leaned over and kicked my feet up on the couch so I was lying down. As my eyes drifted closed, my phone alerted me to an incoming text. It was from Master.

I look forward to it as well. Does tonight work for you?

I don't have to work so it would be perfect.

Send me your address and I'll be there at six to pick you up.

I quickly entered my address and sent it to him before tucking the phone under one arm as I drifted off to sleep. I meant to listen for a return message, but my body had other ideas and I was out cold in seconds.

When I awoke it was definitely past noon from the way the sun shone through the curtains. A glance at the clock let me know I still had hours before John was due to show. Knowing I had a date with nothing except work clothes in my closet, I hurriedly put on clean jeans with a t-shirt and drove to a nearby strip mall, where there were a few boutiques.

It took much longer than I wanted, but I finally found a dress that I felt comfortable yet sexy in. Long, lace sleeves made me feel covered even though there was a low dip in the back of the dress.

After rushing home, I showered before blowing my hair completely straight. Slipping the dress on, I admired it in the mirror for a moment, noting that the mid-thigh length was just sexy enough for me. I knew I didn't have much time left so I hastily put on darker than normal smoky eyeshadow with eyeliner. A dash of mascara and lip gloss finished my look. As I stepped into a pair of four-inch black heels, the door bell rang.

I practically ran to the door, then forced myself to take a deep breath and run a hand through my hair before opening it. There he was.

John was dressed in a perfectly-tailored suit that showed off his lean, muscular body. It was almost sinful simply to look at him, he looked that good. As soon as he saw me, a smile spread over his face and he stepped forward.

"Alix," he said in that husky, delicious voice with a slight British accent.

"John," I fought the urge to look down as my nerves skyrocketed. I had tried not to think about it all day, but I was finally getting the one thing I'd wanted for so long.

"Can I come in?" he asked, yet took another step closer, knowing I wouldn't refuse him.

"Absolutely." I opened the door wider to accommodate his larger frame. Once he was through, I closed it and leaned back, taking deep breaths.

Turning, he faced me and lifted a hand. I thought he was going to touch my face like he did quite often, but instead his fingers lifted the pearl necklace. "They look beautiful on you."

"Thank you." I ducked my head, unable to meet his eyes after such a compliment.

"Are you ready for tonight?" Before I could even answer, he framed my body with his arms and lowered his head until his lips were just above mine. "I have an exciting evening planned, Precious."

"I would ask where we're going, but I have a feeling you won't tell me." I smirked.

"And you would be correct about that. However, part of the fun starts here." Dropping his hands to my shoulders, he slowly trailed them up my neck to cup my face and plant a solid, chaste kiss against my lips. "Turn around, Precious."

Taking one last look into his blue eyes, I turned to face the door.

A large, warm hand traced the opening on the back of my dress as an appreciative hum came from him.

When a cool, heavy material wrapped around my upper arm, I looked down. It was a leather band. What it was for, I didn't know, but I knew I'd be finding out shortly.

A similar band was wrapped around my other arm and something wrapped across the center of my back. I didn't understand until I tried to move my arms forward and found I couldn't.

My upper arms were strapped to my torso. It wasn't tight or painful, just... restrictive. Panic welled inside me, but I pushed it back knowing John wasn't going to hurt me. He only ever introduced me to new levels of arousal and passion.

"Does that feel okay? Not too tight?" John asked as if reading my thoughts.

"Yes, sir. It's fine. Although I will say I'm not sure how I'm going to eat or do other things," I said, concerned.

"Don't worry. I'll take care of everything."

Like I had any doubt. I nearly snorted, but that wouldn't go over well so I forced a smile instead.

John opened the coat closet next to the door and rifled through it before shutting it. "That's all the coats you have? You need to go shopping. I think that'll be one of the things we shall do together."

My cheeks flared pink. I didn't know how to respond. I didn't go out and party or even socialize with people outside of work, so I didn't have much that didn't fall into the "boring work clothes" category.

"Come. I have something that'll work in the car," John said, opening the front door for me.

I turned to grab my purse and phone, but he stepped in my way.

"You won't be needing anything like that tonight. Except your house key." He grabbed my key ring off the counter before placing a hand on my lower back and gently, yet forcefully, showing me out of the house. Locking the door behind us, he rushed to open the passenger door for me before running around and sliding into the driver's seat. I'd never seen a car with doors that open upward and it made me feel like I was climbing into the Delorean in *Back to The Future*. Well, a super nice and fancy one, anyway.

As he drove away from my house, he glanced at me and smiled broadly. "Have I told you how beautiful you are?"

"Yes, thank you." I didn't know how else to address the compliment. I felt like a clumsy, ball of nerves, not beautiful.

The drive passed quickly and quietly. It was possible we were both dealing with nerves or maybe it was that we didn't need meaningless conversation to fill every moment spent together. When we pulled into a parking lot, John parked the car before reaching into the backseat to retrieve a black scarf.

"This will work perfectly," he said before climbing out of the car. Moving briskly, he went around the car to open the door for me. I was thankful since I didn't think I could've managed with the restriction of my arms. John scooped me out of my seat before letting me slide down his body to my feet. As I reeled from the feeling of his body, he wrapped the scarf around my back and shoulders.

I could feel the fabric brush against the opening on my back, telling me that with the way it was wrapped around my shoulders and upper arms it effectively concealed the contraption John had locked me into.

"There we go." John walked a slow circle around me as his eyes took me in from head to toe from every angle. "You look perfect."

With that, he wrapped his arm around my waist and led me toward the restaurant. It wasn't somewhere I'd been before, but from the number of cars in the parking lot I'd say it had to be pretty darn good. John opened the door, letting me walk in before him. His hand only left my back momentarily before it returned. It was like he didn't want to let me get too far from him, which was reassuring since I was limited in what I could and couldn't do. At the hostess stand, John let them know he had a reservation.

"Would you like to check your wrap, miss?" the hostess asked once she found what she needed in the book before her.

"No, she's fine," John answered before I could even open my mouth. Obviously he'd anticipated the question.

"Very well." The hostess gave me a look that clearly stated what she thought about a man answering for his date. I didn't care. I found it kind of attractive that he took the time to consider what would be asked of me. Grabbing a few menus from behind her, the hostess stepped from her stand. "Right this way."

Pressure from John's hand told me he wanted me to walk in front of him, so I did.

"Here we are." The hostess waited for us to take our seats.

John pulled out a chair for me, which I happily sat in. After he took a seat across from me, the hostess laid menus in front of each of us and recited the specials, none of which I paid any attention to. I was more enthralled by the man across the table from me. I'd expected him to request a booth so he could sit next to me and torture me with some sexual game, but he didn't and that only drove me to wonder what he had planned. Nothing with him was left to chance, nothing was a surprise to him. If it was, he played it off as if he'd planned for it.

"I'll be ordering for us both, so no need to figure out how you're going to read the menu." John captured the one in front of me and placed it with his own once the hostess left.

"Come here often?" I asked when he didn't even open his own menu.

"Yes, I suppose you could say that." John shrugged as a waiter appeared with a bottle of wine. After John gave his approval, he poured a single glass before disappearing again.

I could sure use a glass, or five, of wine, but I wasn't going to tell that to John. I didn't want him to know just how nervous I was. To my surprise, John lifted the glass to my lips and tilted it so I could sip from it.

"You wouldn't be able to do it yourself and I'm not drinking tonight," John explained before giving me another sip.

"Should I not be drinking either, sir?" I asked. The fact that he wasn't drinking reinforced my idea that he had other plans for me after the restaurant.

"A glass or two will help relax you. I can tell that you're on edge, and getting you to relax a bit would be a good thing. Although I can tell you, there is absolutely nothing to be worried about. I'm the same person you know and have spent quite a bit of time with." John reached across the table to brush his thumb against my lips. "I want to see you at ease with me the way you once were."

"It's that obvious?" I cringed.

"No, Precious. Most people probably wouldn't even notice, but I know you. I have been with you when you are completely relaxed. *That* is the woman I want. The woman not afraid to show me everything about herself, all the good, all the bad. I want it all. While you are beautiful now, you are breathtaking when you let all those walls come down and I get to see the real woman inside you — the one no one else gets to see."

John's words made me suck in a breath. I didn't know what to say. The pure honesty in his voice, the conviction that he knew exactly what he was talking about without hesitation, without stuttering, made me want to be that person. It made me want to be able to drop my walls, to show him the woman I was all the time. While he'd seen and learned a lot of my secrets, he hadn't managed to learn them all and I wanted to keep it that way. Some things are best left in the deep, dark recesses of one's brain so no one else can be scared by them.

As much as I was attracted to John, I was unable to let go completely and I didn't think I ever would be able to.

Chapter 4

John

I knew she was holding out on me. There was something she didn't want to tell me, but I wasn't going to let her keep any secrets. Well, I would for a bit. Eventually, though, she would share them. It was the only way she was ever going to be able to heal from her addiction and whatever had triggered her to have it. Not everyone had a reason, but from what little she'd told me about it I knew there was *something* in her past. Most people were trying to run from old demons. I knew I was. I had my own closet full of them that haunted me. One day I would have to share them with her, but until she was ready to share hers, my own would be kept locked away.

We would come to that level of trust and security eventually. What I really wanted was to get to know every quirk and curve of her body and personality. The woman under the meek and mild exterior she showed to the world. I'd seen the expressive, sensual woman in our time together with the blindfold, I just had to figure out how to get that same side to show without it.

Looking across the table at Alix was almost surreal. Me. On a date. With Alix. Who would've thought? I hadn't dated much since Mariah and I split. Then much of my time was spent working or checking on Alix.

When the waiter returned I placed our order and he left us alone again. I was a regular. I didn't order the same thing every time, though I'd sampled just about everything on the menu.

Carefully, I lifted the wine glass again for Alix, who sipped from it. I set the glass back on the table between us and really let my eyes take in her face. "Feeling calmer now, beautiful?" I asked. A few sips of wine and some time seemed all she needed to regain her composure.

"Yes, sir. Much better," Alix said as she flashed me a smile. I could tell she was still a bit uncomfortable, but it was likely from the inability to use her arms freely. Then again, that was part of the experience, the unknown.

"Can I tell you my cock is so hard from knowing you are bound right here in the middle of this fancy restaurant, and we are the only people who know? It turns me on like you wouldn't believe to know you are willing to hand over so much control and trust me so much in a public setting." I leaned forward to trace her hair line with my fingertips. "I love knowing you are so dependent upon me to help you."

"Only for you, John." Alix nearly whispered the words, but I felt them soul-deep. I was coming to love the way she found sir, John and Master interchangeable when we were out and about, but when we were playing it was always Master or sir.

"That only makes me cherish it that much more, Precious." Before I could continue, the waiter appeared with our plates of steaming food. After setting them down and refilling the glass of wine, he disappeared again. I grabbed my fork and smirked at Alix. "You see, this would be so much more fun if I pulled out the blindfold I have in my pocket. I won't, though. I like seeing your eyes, since they were hidden from me for so long."

"You have a blindfold with you right now?" Alix lifted an eyebrow in question as her eyes widened.

"I do. It's more of a length of thick black satin than an actual blindfold, but yes, I have one. Would you like me to put it on you?" I wondered if she would go that far in public. It wouldn't bother me to put it on her or sit at the table while people looked. I was more afraid she would clam up than anything. People judged no matter what so I might as well enjoy my life — besides, I'd probably never see them again anyway.

"Uh, no… No." She cleared her throat and shook her head emphatically.

"Damn," I said, biting down on my bottom lip to hide my smile. "Maybe next time."

Cutting into the ravioli on my plate, I lifted a small bite to my mouth to blow on it before reaching across the small table. "Try this. It's my favorite."

As she opened her mouth, she locked eyes with me. She kept them on me as she chewed slowly before swallowing. "Delicious."

"Want more?" I picked up another bite off the plate for her in anticipation.

"Don't you want some?" she asked, dropping her eyes to my lips before they jumped back to mine.

"I'd rather watch you eat it." It was true. I did. Everything she did was sensual and made me want to take her to bed or tie her down and turn her pretty skin turn pink. While we'd only had sex twice, many other acts we had explored were equally amazing.

"Maybe I'd like to watch you enjoy your food as well, Master." Alix's tongue darted out to wet her lips as she wiggled a bit in her chair.

Leaning forward, I rested my elbows on the table and lowered my voice. "Are you turned on, Precious?"

"Yes, sir." Her answer was immediate even as she leaned in to me.

"Mmm. Too bad there is nowhere I could usher you away to help you. I guess you'll have to tough it out," I said. Her low-pitched moan made me smile. I had a small vibrator in my pocket that I planned to slip in her at some point, but it was too early in the night. Plus, I really didn't know of somewhere I could sneak in a private moment. The tables weren't draped with tablecloths for me to use as cover, sadly, so it would have to wait. Sitting back in my seat, I picked up the fork once again. "I guess we'd better finish the meal so we can get going, yes?"

"Yes, sir. Please," Alix whimpered, shifting in her seat again.

I made quick work of the ravioli on my plate, alternating between taking bites myself and feeding Alix. Between bites, I helped her drink the glass of wine as well. Alix was no longer chewing with slow, careful bites, but rapidly, eager to leave. I wasn't going to object and neither was my dick. The damn thing got hard from practically every little thing she did. Add in the restraint barely hiding under the scarf wrapped around her and I wasn't likely to be getting soft anytime soon.

Once we finished the meal, the waiter appeared to take away the mostly-empty plates. "Can I offer you dessert or after-dinner coffee, perhaps?" he asked.

"No," Alix said immediately.

"Yes." I smiled at the hairy-eyed stare Alix flung my way. Hell, I could wait a few more minutes if it ratcheted her up even more. Always so eager to get to the fun part. I would need to teach her some patience. I kept my eyes on her as the waiter proceeded to list the desserts available. It didn't really matter what it was, it was more about the delay.

"The first one," I said not remembering what it was. Once the waiter left, I scratched my cheek and looked around the room before looking back at Alix. "Are you in a rush, Precious?"

"Are you not, sir?" Alix smirked. She had such a spunky personality when she got upset. It was quite attractive as long as she didn't push too far.

"Oh, I'm plenty ready to take you back to our room to show you what else I have planned for the night, but I also like to savor the moment. We will get there eventually and it'll be better for the wait," I explained.

"I'll have to take your word for it, sir. I can't say I enjoy waiting," Alix said.

"I can teach you. In fact, I have taught you already. You've learned to be patient when it comes to release. Have you not?" I leaned back in my seat when the waiter reappeared. I hadn't even realized I was leaning into her, wanting to get closer, until I had to make room for the dessert plate. The waiter scurried away when I handed him a stack of cash for the bill.

"I have." Alix dropped her eyes for a moment before lifting them again. "Thanks to you, sir."

"Exactly. You are capable of much more than you give yourself credit for." I lifted a clean fork and cut into the small slice of cheesecake on the center of the chilled plate. "Have a bite, Precious."

Alix wrapped her lips tightly around the fork tines, making sure to clean as much from it as she could when I pulled the fork from her mouth. "Rich and creamy. Just how I like it." She gave me hooded eyes and a soft smile that let me know she meant the double entendre.

"Mmm. I'll be able to help you out with that a bit later as well," I said, scooping another bite onto the fork for her. After she chewed it, I held up another bite, but she shook her head.

"I'm very full, sir."

"Very well." I ate the bite before returning the fork to the table and standing. "Let's be on our way, then."

I helped Alix get out of the booth, making sure the scarf stayed over her harness. Placing my hand on her lower back, I showed her out of the restaurant and back to my car. As we neared it, I pulled the scarf off her, causing her to gasp.

"What are you..." She trailed off as she turned to face me.

Stepping close to her, I pressed her back against the car and wrapped the scarf around her eyes, securing it behind her head.

"The fun has only begun, Precious," I whispered into her ear. My hand slid into my pocket to retrieve the small vibrator. Dropping my lips to her, I lifted one of her legs which made her dress ride higher, exposing her thigh-highs and the clasps of her garter belt. The hand with the vibrator slipped between her legs. Finding her damp silk panties, I broke the kiss to pant into her ear. "I could fuck you right here. In the parking lot of my favorite restaurant, likely to get caught. You are so damn sexy, Alix."

As she opened her lips to reply, I pushed the tip of the vibrator into her, causing her to clamp her lips closed. Her knees buckled, but I held her firmly against the car with my body. As I pushed the vibrator deeper, she moaned softly as her nails dug into my abdomen.

"Something for later," I said with a soft kiss to her lips before slowly lowering her leg back down. The remote in my pocket would allow me to play at will. It had two parts — the tip rotated to stimulate her g-spot while the base vibrated to tease her pussy and clit. "Get in the car."

I held onto her arm to make sure she could get in without falling. It's surprising how much hands were used without realizing it. Alix was figuring it out though. Once she was seated, I closed the overhead door and took long strides to circle the car quickly. As I sat in the car, I jostled the remote in my pocket and from the jump Alix gave, it started up the vibrator as planned. Reaching over, I pulled the seatbelt across her lap and gave her a brief kiss on the lips.

"How you doing, Precious? Still okay with the arms?" I asked just to be sure.

"Good, sir. It's an interesting experience." She wiggled her fingers as if showing me they were still there. "It's strange and exciting at the same time."

"It's only the beginning," I said, smirking as I navigated the car out of the parking lot and towards Scene.

"I figured as much, sir. You know, with the new, uh, addition," she stuttered and wiggled in the seat a bit. The blindfold didn't seem to bother her at all, though.

"It's best if you don't try to figure out what is planned. I doubt you'll be able to guess anyway." I glanced briefly at her, but kept my eyes on the road. "Although, I suppose the anticipation is good. Keep that pussy ready for me, because I plan to keep it busy. And not only with my cock, as I'm sure you can tell."

As much as I wished it could be my dick in her all night, I was human and it didn't work that way. Luckily, her pussy was much more resilient than my dick was so I could make her come many more times than I did. Pulling up in front of Scene, I parked farther out in the lot than I normally did, giving us a bit of privacy, but still within range of the security cameras in case something were to happen.

I swiftly made my way around the car to help Alix out. As soon as her feet hit the ground, I spun her so her chest was pressed to the cold metal behind the door. Shutting the door next to her, I slid my hand between her hips and the car. Little by little, my fingers caressed the soft skin of her thigh from just above her stockings up until I reached her panties.

"We are going to do something very different tonight." I shoved aside the elastic band so I could slide my fingers across her bare pussy lips, teasing her swollen clit.

"Seems the same to me, sir." Alix gave a smart-ass remark without hesitation.

"Seems my Precious is getting too bold for her own good," I said harshly. Pinching her clit tightly between my fingers, I wrapped my arm around her ribs as her knees weakened. "That mouth of yours is getting a little snarky for my tastes."

"Y… yes, sir," Alix gasped even as her hips rocked against my hand.

The bite of my fingers didn't turn her off. It only pushed her closer to an orgasm. Releasing her clit, I moved my fingers to massage the tiny bud instead of hurting it. "I'll give you two choices. You will get to pick how things will go. The thing is, once you pick, there is no changing your mind. There is no going back. Got it?"

"Mmm, yes," she moaned as she pushed her back against my chest. My cock pressed against her ass and she leaned her head against me.

Kissing her neck while my finger still circled her clit, my voice was rough when I asked, "Excess or Absence?"

"What? That doesn't make sense." Alix lifted her head as confusion set in.

"Pick. One or the other."

"I don't know. Oh…" She whimpered as I increased the pressure on her clit.

"Now," I snarled angrily. My own control was slipping and I needed her to make the choice before I took it from her.

"Absence," she blurted then cried out when I stepped back from her, removing my hands from her body as I did it. "Wait. No. I meant excess. I don't know what they mean, but don't stop!" she pleaded as she turned to look at me.

"Let's go inside and I'll show you." I once again placed my hand on her lower back and urged her toward the club.

Chapter 5

Alix

Spending time with John outside of the club had been much different than I thought it would be. He was still completely dominating, but he smiled and took care of me in ways I hadn't expected. If he hadn't bound my arms, I doubt I would've seen the side of him I had been lucky enough to glimpse. He was sweet and caring while still being incredibly sexy and in charge.

When he pulled his hand from my panties just before I came in the parking lot, I wanted to stomp my foot and demand he continue, but I knew it would get me nowhere with him. If anything it would only have gotten me a punishment. Instead I was left wondering what he had in mind for me that had to do with *absence*. I didn't know why I picked that one over the other option. Maybe because the absence of my orgasm was gnawing at my mind. I needed to get off from all the foreplay at dinner and then him putting that damn vibrator in me and letting it sit there with a low humming sensation since he'd gotten in the car.

As we walked toward the club, the vibrations made me walk with jolting steps, since they were pushing me slowly toward release without my control. John's firm, warm hand on my lower back told me I didn't have a choice but to continue inside. The harness anchoring my arms was in clear view since he'd removed the scarf, not that he seemed worried about it. I tried not to think about the fact that other people would be able to see it, but I still had butterflies in my stomach over it. I didn't like when people stared at me, judged me.

The bouncer at the door opened it for us without a word and we stepped into the small reception area. As usual, there was a finely-dressed woman waiting there.

"Nothing to hand over," John said to the woman before ushering me past the curtains, which he held out of the way for me.

I turned to walk down the hall toward the room John and I always played in, but with his hand, he told me that wasn't where we were going. Instead he directed me into the main room. There weren't many people there, which was a first for me. Every time I had looked in, it had been practically overflowing.

John led me to a chair wide enough to easily seat two. Once he sat, he pulled me into his lap so my legs crossed over his and my back was against the armrest. One of his arms wrapped around my shoulders to play with my hair while the other draped over my lap to rest on my outer thigh. "Since you decided absence would be the punishment, you are not allowed to come for the rest of the night. If you do, you will be punished immediately. Understand?"

"Yes, sir." I swallowed the lump in my throat. There was only so much I could do to keep my body from giving in and I was already on the edge. I knew then and there I would be getting at least one punishment because it was inevitable; I could only hold off so much longer, especially if he built upon the vibrations still coming from the toy in my pussy.

"Good, then stand and strip," he demanded.

I hesitated, since I didn't think it'd be possible to get the tight dress off while having my arms bound the way they were.

John bounced his leg underneath me and, oddly, the vibrations grew stronger from the toy. "That's the only warning you'll get tonight. Do as I say, Precious."

Clenching my teeth, I managed to maneuver myself off his lap. After wiggling my shoulders to see how much room I had, I sighed and lowered my head.

"Sir, I can't do it on my own." I looked up through my lashes at him, in hopes he would understand, while trying to ignore my growing arousal.

"Exactly. You need me to help you. Turn around," John said, spreading his thighs so I could step between them. His hands were quick to unhook the harness and release my arms. To my surprise, he helped me rotate each shoulder a few times, making sure the circulation was okay after such a long time being restricted. "Now, do as I said."

Facing him again, I immediately pulled the top down to my waist, exposing my breasts to him and the rest of the room. A brief glance around told me no one appeared to even notice. Pushing the material off my hips, I revealed the garter belt, thigh highs and black silk panties that had been underneath.

"Sexy," John breathed as his hands came to rest on my hips. Lifting me, he moved me back onto his lap. "That's much better. So much easier to play with."

His arm wrapped around my back as his head lowered to a breast, sucking the nipple into his hot mouth. Clenching my thighs together, I tried to hold back the orgasm that threatened. It didn't help since it only pushed the toy deeper and made the vibrations more pointed; whatever was rubbing against my g-spot moved to be right where I needed it.

Squeezing my eyes closed and biting my lip, I dropped my head back and the orgasm washed over me as John sank his teeth into my tender breast tissue. When I opened my eyes again, I was light-headed and breathing hard… and John was looking right into my eyes.

"You know what that means, don't you?" His voice was deep and sinful; his accent had gotten thicker. Standing, he set me on my feet as well. His hand wrapped around the back of my neck as he forcefully showed me to one of the empty little stages. "Bend. Now."

I lowered my chest to the cold wooden table, which reminded me of the first time John had brought me to this room, but I'd been blindfolded then.

"Tell me why you are here," John barked.

"I came," I said, closing my eyes. I'd known it was going to happen, but it didn't make it easier to admit I hadn't followed his instructions. I hated disappointing him.

"And what happens when you come, Precious?"

I heard the tinkling of what sound like a belt buckle. "I get punished, sir."

"Exactly. This time you will only get five. Count out loud for everyone to hear." John's hand ran up my back before slithering down again.

I could tell from the position of his hand that he'd stepped to my side, but I refused to open my eyes to know for certain. I had no other warning before the loud slap of leather meeting skin filled my ears. The intense burning sensation immediately followed from where his belt had landed on my ass.

"One, sir," I gasped. Tears instantly sprang to my eyes from the pain.

Again the loud clap and the burning sensation, only lower on my ass.

"Two, sir," I said, digging my fingers into my palms, fighting the urge to move. It wasn't the most intense thing John had done, but there had been very little warning which made it seem worse some how.

Slap, and burning sprang up on the very bottom of my cheeks.

"Three, sir," I shouted as anger sprouted in me. I hadn't been allowed enough time to prepare myself.

Fingers dug into my hair, yanking my head back before I felt cloth against my ass making me whimper. John leaned over my back, digging his hips into my ass. "You don't get to be angry. This is your punishment. You were told the rules. You broke them. You want it to stop, say the word. Hell, tell me to stop and I will. Is that what you want? You want me to stop? I stop now, you walk out of here by yourself."

"No, sir. Sorry, sir," I groaned when he sucked my earlobe between his teeth.

"That's what I thought. Watch your anger, Precious, or I'll give you a reason to be angry." And just that fast, he was gone again. Sucking in a deep breath, I pressed my head to the lacquered wood.

The next two slaps were harder than before and over the first ones, which made them burn worse, but I managed to utter the numbers even as tears rolled down my cheeks.

As soon as my punishment was over, he helped me stand before scooping me into his arms and returning to where we'd been originally. Sitting, he placed me on the leather next to him. It was cold and felt amazing on my hot skin. His thumb and forefinger pinched my chin, turning me to face him.

"Do you understand why I had to do that?" he asked, keeping his eyes on mine as his palm dropped to rest on my thigh.

"Because I went against your rules," I answered, but it was halfhearted. I wanted to leave. Things had taken an unexpected turn and I didn't like where it was going.

"Yes and no. What we have between us is more than rules. It's *so* much more than that. Don't you get it? It's about learning to control your body and its reactions. It's not about coming when I told you not to. It is about being able to know when enough is enough and voicing it. *Let me know* when things are too much or when I'm pushing you too hard. *Speak up* if I'm doing something you don't like." Pulling me so I was straddling his lap, he put in me a position where I was looking down at him. "Did I think you wanted to be spanked? No, but you needed a reminder of who is in charge and why you listen to what I tell you. It's not just about when you can come, but everything. It is my job to take care of you and I take it very seriously. Sometimes, though, it is your job to protect yourself. As much as I want to always be with you, I can't. It's just not possible, so I need to know that you will be okay without me right there."

"I can take care of myself." I stiffened my back. I felt like we were having two different conversations. How things went from spanking and coming to taking care of myself, I didn't quite understand.

"Control, Precious. Learn to control your body and you don't have to worry about that part of life anymore. You can be more free. You can stop worrying about what other people think because it doesn't matter. Me and you. *We* are what matter." John lowered his forehead to my chest as he breathed deeply. "Now that you are mine, I worry someone will try to take you. That someone will try to use the S and M relationship we have to pry you from my arms."

It made me smile as I ran a hand through his hair. "Master, that's not going to happen. I don't always understand what we have, but I can tell you it's not as flimsy as you worry. The connection we share is much more than most people ever experience once in their life. At this point, you should worry I'll never let you go."

A rumble vibrated from his chest before he leaned back in the chair. "You are too perfect. Take off my shirt."

"Gladly, sir." Happy to seemingly have gotten through an awkward conversation, I rapidly pried the tiny buttons on his dress shirt open. My anger at having been disciplined was gone. Once I reached the top of his pants, he moved to shrug out of his jacket before stopping and looking as if he was in thought. I nearly yelped in surprise when he put me at his side again on the cool leather.

"Change in plans. Come, Precious," John stated as he snatched my dress from the floor.

I rushed to stand and follow him as he swiftly moved toward the way we'd come in. My heart started to flutter in panic at the thought of him taking me outside while nude, but thankfully, he turned to go down the hallway. When I made it into the room, I was surprised to find him undoing his own cufflinks as he stepped out of his shoes.

"Everything off." He barely looked up at me as he proceeded to strip himself.

Following directions, I carefully removed my garter belt, panties and thigh highs.

John approached me with calculated steps before reaching out to grab the only thing I had left on. My pearl necklace. Hooking a finger in it, he led me to the dresser next to the bed.

"Open the second drawer," John said as he released my necklace and took a step back.

Slowly, I raised a trembling hand to the drawer's handle. I had never seen inside any of the drawers so it made me scared to think exactly what I was going to be retrieving. The further open I pulled the drawer, the more calm I became. There was nothing I hadn't at least seen before.

"Pick up the nipple clamps."

Carefully, I grasped the small metal clamps between a finger and thumb of each hand. There was a long metal cord between them. I turned around to face him and held my hands out toward him.

"Mmm, yes, I think these are exactly what we need. Now get on all fours." John took the clamps from me, clenching them in one hand.

I didn't know what to say. I'd never played with anything that looked like those. They looked painful and I'd already experienced enough pain for the night. My mind was spiraling out of control, trying to stay caught up with all that was going on. Sure, he'd done worse, but it was so much different to have my sight to go with the experience.

I did as he asked, lowering myself to all fours and closing my eyes. Instantly, I felt a rush of calm come over me. I was hyping myself up, twisting things into something they weren't, all because I was afraid.

To my surprise, Master's fingers slipped into my body. Unfortunately, it was only to retrieve and remove the small toy that was still vibrating. Master tossed it onto the bed before returning his attention to me. "On your knees only, Precious."

I pushed off the ground to rest my butt against my crossed feet. As much as I dreaded what he had in mind, I wanted it. He never failed to make sure I enjoyed our time together. It was me who had to remember nothing had changed.

John stepped in front of me, the chain dangling between his spread hands. He dropped to his knees in front of me, making my eyes widen since I'd never seen him on his knees.

I thought he was going to kiss me as he closed the distance between us, but at the last second he dipped his head to suck a nipple into his mouth. Once he got it perked up and begging for more, the bite of the metal clamp came; I squeezed my eyes shut and tried to mentally push away the pinching sensation. Thankfully, it only seemed to last a few seconds, but he was already teasing my other nipple to a peak. Clamping down on my second nipple, he stood again and held a hand down to help me to my feet.

"Now, we will go back out to the main room."

Chapter 6

John

As much as I wanted to play with Alix, hearing her tell me she wasn't going to let me go nearly made me fuck her right there. Not that I wouldn't do such a thing, but I had other plans for her and I couldn't lose control, not yet. I had told her it was going to be a night of absence and I planned to fully see it through.

Alix looked breathtaking in her garter belt, but she nearly stopped my heart standing naked in front of me. I stalked toward her once I disrobed completely. Hooking my finger into the pearls around her neck, I used the delicate strand as a leash to lead her to the drawer. Simply seeing them on her made me hard and had my heart thumping harder against my ribs. *She was mine.*

Once I was holding the nipple clamps I had her take from the dresser, I told her to get on all fours. Not a position I put her in often, out of respect. Plus, now that we'd lost the blindfold I wanted to see as much of her as possible. My little flirt lifted her luscious ass, showing me her beautiful pussy between her thighs. The sight had my cock throbbing and releasing a single drop of pre-come.

Kneeling behind her, I dipped two fingers into her to snag the toy that hadn't yet been used to its full capability. I

52

would have to use it another time since it was normally so fun to have her pleasure in the palm of my hand, literally. Once I disposed of the toy, I stood again and moved in front of her.

Letting the length of chain slip through one hand into the other, which was still damp from retrieving the toy, I stretched the nipple clamps between my hands before standing and walking around her to kneel in front of her.It would've been simple enough to make her stand while I attached the clamps, but I wanted her to know this was more than a power play. Plus, since I hadn't used the clamps on her before, I wanted her lower to the ground in case she passed out. Getting on the bed was out of the question because once we got in it, I'd be in her without a doubt. So I was improvising.

Lowering my head closer to her, I thought about pressing my lips to hers just as she dragged her tongue over the bottom one. Instead, I sucked one of her nipples into my mouth to prepare it for the clamp. Quickly, I slipped the clamp on; she barely responded, so I wasted no time in getting the other one on. The silver chain dangled between her breasts.

I stood and held a hand down to help her to her feet as well. A glance to the clamped flesh, I licked my lips in delight. Her nipples had turned dark red from the pressure they were exerting on the delicate flesh and it reminded me of how her skin looked after a good spanking.

"Now, we will go back out to the main room." I smiled when she lifted her head in question. "Or we could stay here. Although, if we stay in here, you will still be held to no orgasms without punishment."

"Very well, sir."

"Well, which would you prefer?" I asked, wanting her to make the choice.

"I want to do whichever would make Master happiest," she whispered, looking into my eyes. I nodded. I knew she'd prefer staying in the room, just the two of us, but I also wanted her to learn not to be so afraid of being around others, of being judged or looked upon.

"We will return to the main room for a bit before I take you home," I said before looping a finger through the chain that linked the clamps and pulling lightly on it. She was quick to follow behind me before it tugged too hard on her nipples. When we returned to the room, it was busier and I was nude with her, which I hoped help bring her some comfort even with the increased activity.

I could tell she was still uneasy about the whole night. She was having a hard time with everything now that she could see, but I would do my best to help her realize that seeing only made things so much more pleasurable. It only added one more sense to the scene. She was beautiful and it was time she realized people wouldn't watch in disgust, but admiration and quite possibly jealousy that I had managed to make her mine.

When I'd first asked her on the date, I hadn't planned on bringing her to the club, but I wanted her to see we could work both in and out of the club at the same time, from one to the other and back again without any awkward or unpleasant moments. I needed her to see what we had was so much more than a dominant and submissive relationship. I wanted her with me all the time, not only for sex. So far, my plan seemed to be working. I was determined to get back the woman she had been when she'd been forced to wear a blindfold at all times while around me. The woman who had few limitations in how far she was willing to go for the sake of pleasure and fulfillment she couldn't find anywhere else.

Locating an empty seat, I pulled her into my lap, her back to my chest so we could both watch the couple using the St. Andrew's Cross. I wasn't interested in what they were doing, but instead in the sounds they were producing, since Precious seemed to be easily stimulated by sounds more than sight. I wanted her to link the two together.

"What scares you most about people watching you, Alix?" I asked as I dragged my tongue up the side of her neck, breathing in her scent, savoring her taste.

"That they can see through all the barriers I've built," she whispered and pressed back against me. My cock was pushed between her tight cheeks and although she sounded scared, I could also feel the moisture from her on my thigh.

"What are you so afraid they'll see?" I wrapped my arms around her, dipping one hand between her thighs while the other massaged a breast.

"That I'm a fake…" She trailed off and dropped her chin to her chest. "That I'm not what I appear to be, that I'm really a broken person deep inside."

I took a moment to digest her words. They were insightful even if she hadn't meant them to be. Anger flared hot inside me at whoever had made her feel so badly about herself. If I could ever get her to tell me, I'd be on the hunt to make that person pay for damaging such a special, delicate woman.

"Do you think not being perfect makes you any less of a person? Any less beautiful or intelligent than anyone else? Everyone had something bad in their past they've had to deal with. They are no better than you unless you give them that control." I pushed my fingers through her pussy lips to slide two fingers into her. The couple on the stage had started their scene and added moans of lust to our hushed conversation.

"It's how I learned to deal with it, to hide from it." She arched her back and spread her legs farther, welcoming me into her body. Her eyes were focused on what was going on before us.

"I don't want you to hide from me. Ever. I want you to know I can be trusted with all your secrets, all your pain. I am here to help you deal with them and no longer fear them." I brushed my lips against her ear as I spoke. My fingers thrust in and out of her as she rotated her hips around them.

"I don't want to hide from you, sir. I want to share every part of myself, but I am scared. Not of you. I'm scared of myself. I've tried facing my past and all it did was make things worse. It's easier to try to forget it ever happened. Try to live with what I have left instead of lose more."

I was impressed she was still so coherent and responsive to our conversation when it was clear her body was fully involved with what I was doing with my fingers, plus the added stimulation of the couple who were fucking on the stage. Then again, it was likely that with all the distractions going on, she didn't realize how much she was sharing with me. That had been part of the reason I had wanted to share such a personal talk around others. It helped me peel back some of her protective shield without her realizing she was lowering her guard.

"Then wait. Wait until you trust me enough to know I will be there to stop things from getting worse. Trust me to support you and protect you because that is all I want, Precious," I murmured against her skin as I breathed in her scent. Deciding I'd pushed enough for one night, I shifted my focus back to the stage. "I want you to watch that couple, hear the couple's moans."

"Yes, sir," she gasped, and it was like she finally realized what she was watching. She tightened around my fingers and I increased the speed at which they were thrusting into her.

"Does it excite you to watch other people having sex? Do you like hearing them moan from pleasure?" I tugged on the chain connected to her nipples causing her to whimper.

"Yes. I never thought I would, but with you touching me, it's incredibly sexy," she answered, leaning her head back against my shoulder.

"Do you want me to fuck you where other people can watch and hear us? Hear how good I make you feel?"

"Mmm, yes." I think she surprised even herself with her answer as her eyes fluttered closed before opening again.

"One day soon, I will take you without the blindfold so you can see the lust you inspire in others while I give you everything you need in front of them. Not tonight though. Tonight you aren't allowed to come, which is such a tragedy. If only you'd picked excess, you could be on the other side, experiencing as many orgasms as I could give you until you begged me to stop and even then I would give you more." I pressed my lips to her head and bucked my hips against her ass letting her know how willing I was to do just that.

Her body started trembling around me and her muscles clenched tighter on my fingers telling me she was on the brink of release, so I pulled my fingers from her on a sigh. Orgasm deprivation could be so sweet and torturous at the same time. I was used to denying myself pleasure, but she was not and having that control over her thrilled the side of me that survived on control.

A whimper left her throat but for once she didn't say anything to try to encourage me to continue. She knew how the game was going to go.

I sat with her fluids running down my legs from how turned on she was as I played with her breasts and we watched the couple continue to fuck. My cock ached to be the one doing the fucking, but I liked waiting. Part of me liked knowing it was me in control, not the beast who hung between my legs, although from time to time he took over.

Slowly I circled her nipples and tugged on the chain, making her cry out. A smile spread over my face — that was one sound I couldn't get enough of.

The couple on stage finally climaxed and the Dom helped his sub off the stage. It wasn't long before another couple took their place. It was a female dominant and her male submissive. She swiftly restrained him to the cross and I could tell from the shift of Alix's hips she was intrigued by the new pairing. I didn't think she'd seen a female top a male in the club before.

"Never seen a Domme?" I asked to be sure. She shook her head and sat up straighter; surely she didn't want to miss a thing since it was new to her. Always curious, my Precious was. Walking around her sub, the Domme slapped at the man's erection, making him moan.

"Doesn't that hurt?" she asked, shocked.

"Sure, but he likes it too. Just like you enjoy when I slap your pussy or your ass," I shrugged, thinking it was the best comparison I could give. She sat forward when the Domme unrolled a whip and stepped far back from her sub. I wanted to laugh at how excited she was to watch, and not in the normal way. I didn't think she was turned on, but more interested to learn about the whip.

The entire time the Domme whipped her sub and he cried out, Alix didn't move. She was entranced. When the Domme put on a strap-on, the spell was broken and she leaned back on my chest.

"I don't think I'd like the whip, sir," she said softly.

"You have nothing to worry about there. It's not something I enjoy myself. There are many other methods to bring pain and pleasure that are much more efficient to me." I rubbed up and down her arms, reassuring her. Really, my biggest issue was that a whip required so much space between the Dom and sub when I'd rather be close while administering pain. It allowed me to make sure my sub was on the same wavelength I was. Less chance of going too far. Plus, it took a lot longer to heal from the open wounds that whips tended to leave behind. I didn't want to not be able to play how I pleased when I pleased.

As the Domme took her sub with the dildo she'd strapped on, Alix moaned with the sub as he arched his back, begging for more from his mistress. Again it was the sounds of others' pleasure that did it for her, but she was watching closely so maybe it was starting to also be the sight of watching others as well.

Adjusting her on my lap, I made her spread her legs over both my thighs and my cock slipped between her legs to glide along her slippery folds. My hands held onto her hips and hers came down to grip my wrists as I rotated her over my cock, letting it bump against her swollen clit in the process.

She seemed to have completely forgotten we were both nude and that pleased me. I wanted her uninhibited side, all rational thought gone as she simply gave herself to me because I wanted her to.

Soon she was rotating her hips with mine and arching against me, begging me for more. It wasn't enough friction to get her off, but it was turning her on to feel me slide against her. One moment I was pushing against her and the next I was in her. I hadn't meant for it to happen, but the angle had been perfect. My heart raced having her clamp down on me, but I couldn't stop. I couldn't pull out of her, not since I was in her and she was still rotating her hips with wild abandon.

Yanking her back, I pushed a hand against her shoulder blades, making her lean forward. Her hands braced against my knees as I thrust up into her at the same time my hands forced her to rock against me.

"Yes, just like that, Precious," I groaned. I reached around and tugged on the chain between her breasts and she pushed harder back against me. My other hand slid up her back to sink into her hair and yank her head back.

"Oh, Master," she cried out, but continued to move as much as she could against me.

With a glance, I saw the couple on the stage was really going at it and I was determined to have my sub making just as much, if not more noise than hers.

"Yeah, tell me how good it feels," I instructed Alix.

"I love having your cock fill me, sir. It's so hard and feels so good stretching me. You make me so wet with the way you control me," she cried out loudly. Knowing she had dropped all her walls and was giving me all of herself had my balls drawing up and my cock throbbing even more. Nothing turned me on like having Alix submit to me and hand me all that she was.

A few thrusts later and I couldn't hold back much longer. I reached up and unclipped one of Alix's nipples and she cried out while clenching down on me. When I did the other side she screamed and I lost it. Wrapping my arm around her waist, I held her down as I thrust erratically against her until I spilled inside of her.

I sucked Alix-scented air into my lungs as I tried to center myself again. She leaned back with me, breathing hard herself.

"I didn't come, Master," she said proudly as I gently rubbed my fingers over her stomach.

"You are such a good girl. I'll have to reward you later for it," I sighed contentedly until I felt my softening cock sliding out of her. Both of us groaned deeply when the last of it slipped free. It took me a few minutes to finally have the strength to move again, but when I did, I helped Alix to her feet. "Come, my love, we are done here for tonight."

I scooped the nipple clamps off the floor before clasping Alix's hand with my opposite one. After a brief stop in my room to redress, I threaded our fingers together and we returned to my car. The ride to her house was more relaxed than the one to the restaurant had been, at least for me.

Once we were inside her place, she locked the door and leaned back on it.

"Would you like a drink? A glass of wine perhaps?" she asked, wringing her hands together. How she reverted back to the shy woman amazed me.

"A glass of water or juice would be great. You can have wine if that is what you prefer," I said. As tempting as it would be to have a glass of wine for what I had in mind, one drink was one too many in my world. When she left the room, presumably to go to the kitchen, I walked through her house. I knew exactly where her bedroom was so I headed there.

By the time she found me, I had run a hot bath and lit the few candles I could find.

"What's this?" She looked around as she held out a glass of what appeared to be grape juice for me. In her other hand was a glass of wine for herself.

I set my glass on the counter before wrapping my arms around her.

"This is the next part of our date," I murmured before taking her lips.

Chapter 7

Alix

I squeezed my glass of wine as John kissed me deeply. While the kiss was passionate, it was slow and tender. I swooned into it. He'd never kissed me quite like that before.

He pulled back, took my glass from me and set it on the counter next to his before reaching up to pull my dress off. It pooled around my feet and he took a step back to look at me, really look at me. He took his time running his eyes over my body. Finally he held out a hand and helped me step out of my dress.

Taking his time, he helped me out of each of my undergarments, which I had hastily put back on before we left the club. When I was naked, he motioned for me to get in the tub. He guided me into the scalding water, and I gasped at its heat. I loved that even though he could be so demanding and unrelenting, he also had a sweet, tender side. He always made sure I was getting everything I needed before I could even ask for it.

"It'll feel good once you're all the way in. Trust me," he said, smiling.

"I do," I answered automatically, because I did. There might be certain things I wasn't willing to share yet, but I did trust him more than I ever had before. Sinking down into the tub, I held my breath, but once it was up to my shoulders I relaxed and blew out a long, calming breath. "You were right."

"I know." He stripped himself before climbing in behind me. The water nearly overflowed, but I didn't care. Let it ruin the whole room, it'd be worth feeling John pressed against me, massaging my shoulders and arms while he kissed the sensitive skin of my neck.

Slowly I felt every single muscle in my body relax from the heat and his ministrations. His hands slowly cupped my breasts before teasing my nipples. Moaning, I arched against him and felt his arousal against my back. One hand slid down my stomach until he reached my clit. Moving in a lazy circle, he teased the nerve-filled bud until I was moving against him, trying to get him to go faster.

"No, Precious, slow. This is going to last," he breathed against my damp skin. Still he moved calmly, farther down, until his fingers found my opening and pressed inside me. His free hand moved to tease my other nipple while his fingers found a leisurely pace gliding in and out of me.

It was exactly what I needed, where I needed it. Biting my lip, I tried to hold back my moans and hide that I was close to the edge, but again, he knew my body as well as I did and pulled out of me.

"Get out of the water," he instructed me, then lifted me under my arms until I pushed my feet under myself and stood. Grabbing a towel, I wrapped it around myself before turning to give him a confused look. He followed me out and slung one around his hips. Without a word, he grabbed my hand and tugged me into my bedroom. Once we were next to the bed, he removed both our towels.

I climbed onto the center of the bed and lay on my back, knowing that was how he liked me. Smiling, he crawled onto the foot and spread my feet apart. His smile grew wider as he looked up the center of my body to meet my gaze. Having his eyes on me while his beautiful face lit up set me on fire. My pussy was crying out from not being allowed to get off. I had to fight to now writhe my hips as need coursed through me when my eyes dropped to his erection that begged for attention.

"Beautiful. Every single inch," he said, lowering his head between my thighs. His tongue slid all the way up my crease and he looked at me again. Licking his lips, he said, "So delicious."

I fisted my hands in the sheets, knowing I could never hold off an orgasm when his mouth was on me — he was too good. Unlike every other time, though, he took his time licking every inch of me before dipping between my swollen lips and teasing my clit, then my opening and even my rosette before moving back up to the top of my slit.

He'd barely touched me and I was already breathing fast. When he sucked my clit into his mouth, I convulsed from the sudden shot of pleasure that came from the single point of my body. He gently flicked the swollen nub as two fingers pressed into me. Just like everything else, they moved slowly in and out, tormenting me.

I didn't think I could take anymore. Thankfully, he seemed to sense it and moved up my body. He stopped to trace my nipples with the tip of his tongue before finally bringing his mouth to mine. My lips parted instantly and I could taste myself on him.

Shifting his hips, his erection found my opening and slowly entered me. Pushing off the mattress, he shifted his hips against mine and even though I tried to align our bodies, he made sure it he didn't slip in me. As he looked down at me, one of his hands slipped down to position himself at my entrance and he smiled. He decided when. His finger flicked against my clit before his hand moved up to cup my cheek. Slowly, he rocked against me and I wrapped my legs around his calves and tightened my arms around his back. Once his balls rested against my ass, he stopped to slow steady movements.

"You feel so good, Precious," he sighed before pressing a soft kiss to my lips.

"Yes, but it's not enough," I groaned. I didn't care if I got another punishment, I needed to come.

"But it is. Relax and leave it to me."

"I'm trying," I whimpered. I could never get off with slow and easy. It had to be hard and fast to get anywhere.

"No, you just think you are. Calm your mind. Trust me to give you what you need," he said, his warm breath mingling with mine while his weight pressed into me.

Taking a deep breath of my own, I thought only of John and our night together, him sliding in and out of me, his body against mine. I felt it then, the building of an orgasm. As soon as I focused on it, it disappeared and I let out a frustrated groan.

"I can't."

"Try again. You can." His voice held so much patience and love I couldn't help but listen.

When I felt the gathering of pleasure, I ignored it as best I could and stayed focused on his slow thrusts and the friction of my nipples against his chest. The look in his eyes as he gazed down at me. The trust, the acceptance that I'd never found anywhere else, it was all right there.

"Come, Precious," John said, and I did. I exploded around him. My nails dug into the flesh of his back, my eyes clenched closed as every muscle tightened painfully before releasing into a completely relaxed state. "Good girl."

As I recovered from my racing heart and rapid breathing, I found John kneeling over my chest. His hand slid up and down his length as he waited for me to float back down.

"Suck me off. Coat your throat with me. Mark it as mine." His eyes glowed in the dim light. He was only inches from my face. Taking a moment, I took a mental picture of him with his hand riding his cock as he stared at me. It was

69

me that turned him on that much and a spark of happiness shot through my entire body.

Licking my lips, I lifted my head and took him into my mouth. My cheeks hollowed as I sucked his erection as deep as I could. Cradling his balls in one hand, I wrapped the other around the base of his cock, the part I couldn't get in my mouth because of the angle. It only took a few strokes before he fisted his hand in my hair and shouted my name as come spurted down my throat.

"God, I think I love you," John said still breathing hard as he moved back down the bed to pull me so I rested on his heaving chest.

"No, you love my body," I joked, resting a hand under my chin as I looked up at his face, but he didn't smile or respond, simply met my gaze for a moment.

"Maybe," he finally whispered. He tucked my head into his chest and murmured, "Sleep, Precious."

I couldn't help but do as I was told. I was exhausted, but it had certainly been a night to remember.

In the morning, I was surprised to find John still wrapped around me. I hadn't expected him to stay the whole night. Running a hand down his stubble-lined cheek, I smiled. I still couldn't believe he was in my bed. As much as I wanted to enjoy him the way he was, I feared he needed to go to work.

"John?" I whispered, stroking his cheek again.

"Precious." His lips barely moved and his eyes stayed closed.

"John? Do you need to work today?" I asked, even though I still wasn't sure he was awake.

He groaned and opened his eyes. It was the first time I'd ever seen him pout. Pulling me closer to him, he rolled onto his back while glancing at the clock.

"Yes, unfortunately. I'm late already, but I really don't want to go," he spoke into my hair as he ran a hand over it.

"Well, as much as I don't want you to leave, you better get a move on. I don't want you to get in trouble with your boss." I sat up and the sheet fell to my lap exposing my breasts.

"That is *not* the way to motivate me to go to work." His eyes were locked on my hard nipples. Licking his lips, he moved toward me, but I jumped out of the bed.

"Come on. None of that," I laughed when his pout reappeared. "I'll see you after you are done at work."

He let out a long, resigned sigh before climbing from the bed. His cock stood erect, but he didn't seem to notice as he scratched his stomach and stretched.

"I'll call you later," he said, wrapping a hand around me before I could dodge him again. He bit my lip then gave me a tender kiss before releasing me again. As he gathered his clothes and put them on, he watched me. "I could get used to waking up next to you."

"Me too," I smiled and wrapped a robe around my nude body. After another kiss, he left and I fell onto the bed to relive the entire night in my head.

Chapter 8

John

I'd never been a morning person, but being roused by Alix seemed to have changed that. After a quick stop at my apartment to shower, I headed to the office. Since I was late, I knew I'd have a couple upset patients to deal with, but it also reinforced the fact that I needed a receptionist. So after calling everyone and letting them know I was running late, I made the call I'd been putting off.

"Hello?" her overly sweet voice carried over the line after only one ring.

"Mariah? It's John." I didn't want to beat around the bush.

"Well, hello John. How are you?" A smile evident in her voice.

"Very well. I'm calling about your application for my receptionist position. I'd like to hire you, if you are still interested." It wasn't a social call and I didn't want her to mistake it as one. I knew I'd have to make sure she knew this wasn't a sign that we were going to, or even could, get back together, but simply the fact that I needed a reliable receptionist.

"When would you like for me to start?" she asked after a moment of quiet.

"As soon as you are available."

"I can be there tomorrow morning, if that works." Her voice had turned to her business tone. Her sickly sweet, over affectionate tone was gone and the unease in my gut settled. Everything would be fine.

"Perfect. You remember where my office is?"

"Yes."

"Then I'll see you at eight sharp," I said, then hung up the phone.

I wasn't sure it was a good idea hiring an ex, but I didn't have much of a choice if I wanted to spend as much time as I could with Alix. I needed the help and she was the only applicant who I thought would work out. Hopefully letting her know where I stood from the get go would make sure she stayed professional. Things had ended amicably so I was sure I had nothing to worry about.

The rest of the day was spent meeting with clients and talking about their problems. In-office hours were normally pretty tame. It was my out-of-office appointments that were more exciting and provided the challenge I loved.

As much as I wanted to run over to Alix's place as soon as I was done with work, I didn't. I wanted to make her wait, allow her time to really let everything sink in. Okay, I did go over, but I didn't knock on the door; I simply checked on her to make sure she was okay before returning home.

I managed to stay away for a whole week, making excuses about work keeping me busy. While I *was* busy getting Mariah brought up to date, it normally wouldn't have kept me from Alix. I'd get glimpses and flirty eye contact when she was at work and I used that to carry me through. I needed to make sure she understood what she was getting into with me and accepted it as her own decision, not something I forced on her.

Through our many text and phone conversations, she more than reassured me she wanted to move forward with everything we could become. She even went so far as to tell me she was scared because she hadn't been in a relationship in a long time, but she wasn't going to let it stop her from exploring what it was we had between us.

On her next day off, I asked to pick her up once I was done working for the day and she said she'd be waiting. I took a shower, then stood in my closet with nothing on looking at all the suits hanging there. Finally I decided on my favorite one. I could've picked jeans, but I liked the way it felt to have a impeccably-tailored pair of trousers with a coat that emphasized my hard-earned body. Plus, I knew Alix couldn't help but drool when I wore them and I loved to tease her every possible way I could.

When I knocked on her door, I wasn't left waiting. She immediately opened it to reveal her beautiful hair was left down, like I preferred. The tight, white dress had to have been something she bought just for me because I didn't think she'd wear it to work. I could see the faint outlines of black lace under it which had my cock throbbing before I'd even said a single word to her.

"John," she said on a breathless sigh.

"Alix." I clasped one of her hands, bringing it up to my lips to leave a soft kiss on her knuckles. "Are you ready?"

"Yes, sir." She held up a ring with her house keys on it, showing me she had been waiting, exactly like she'd said she would be.

We passed the drive to dinner with idle chatter. The meal was filled with the same. It was nice to have someone to talk to about mundane things. I still hadn't told her Mariah was my ex, but I didn't think it was an issue since on her first day I had made it as clear as I could that she was only there to do a job and that was it. She'd been professional ever since.

I loved hearing about Alix's day even though it was filled with cleaning and chores around the house. She told me stories about Jennifer, the girl that worked the receptionist desk at the hotel, and had us both laughing at her theatrics.

By the time I pulled up at the club I was more than ready to get her out of the slinky dress that'd kept me half hard all night and hear her moans that I'd missed all week.

Once we walked into the club, I hooked a finger through her pearl necklace and led her to my room. I shut and locked the exterior door before closing the one to the dressing area just outside the room. There were to be no interruptions.

Taking her in my arms, I unzipped her dress while my lips met hers. Our tongues tangled as I pushed her dress off, letting it pool around her feet.

"May I undress you, Master?" she asked, removing her lips from mine.

"You may," I said, stepping back.

Her hands slid up my chest to shove my coat over my shoulders. It slid down my arms to fall to the floor.

"I remembered this time," she murmured, reaching for my cufflinks next. She hastily undid them and they joined my coat. Ever so slowly, her hands glided up my arms and over my shoulders to the top button on my shirt. One at a time, she released each button until she got to where the shirt was tucked into my slacks. Instead of yanking it out of them, she simply moved to the clasp on my trousers and had them falling around my shoes before continuing with the shirt.

Dropping to her knees, she untied my shoes and I helped her remove them and my socks as I stepped from my trousers at the same time. I shrugged out of my shirt as she returned to her feet with a shy smile on her face.

"I would've helped you with that, sir." Her hands ran over my shoulders and down my arms as if she were removing the shirt that was no longer there. Once she got to my hands, she pulled them to her waist and released them.

"All done, sir. Thank you for letting me assist you in undressing. It brings me great pleasure to do so."

I loved when she admitted she liked submitting to me, doing things to help me that I could have easily done on my own, but I especially liked having her hands and attention on me. Tugging her against my chest, I unbuckled her bra and let her shrug the straps off her shoulders.

"Well done, Precious. Now go to your square and wait for me." I watched as she dropped her bra and moved to kneel on the padded square that wouldn't hurt her knees as badly as the hard floor. She spread her knees, her hands resting on her thighs, her head down as her hair fell around her beautiful body.

I went to the dresser and removed the blindfold I'd used on her numerous times along with a pair of handcuffs she hadn't seen before. Stepping in front of her, I dangled the cloth where she could see it and I heard her draw in a sharp breath.

"While I absolutely love seeing your eyes, I need you to wear the blindfold for a bit tonight. Do you understand?" I trailed the edge of the satin cloth over her shoulder as I moved behind her.

"Yes, sir," she said, just loud enough for me to hear.

"Are you afraid of the blindfold?" I asked, hearing uncertainty in her voice.

"No, sir. I've gotten used to not wearing it," she answered as she straightened her back.

"You will enjoy it. Trust me," I whispered in her ear as I wrapped the cloth around her face, covering her eyes. "Stand."

She pushed to her feet and moved her hands behind her back to clasp them together.

Using the edge of one cuff, I trailed it from her shoulder down her arm before linking it around one wrist, pulling it around to her front as I pressed my chest to her back. Grabbing her other wrist, I moved it to join the first one and cuffed it as well. The cuffs were real ones, not the play kind you could buy at novelty stores. They were heavy and inescapable without a key. This wasn't a game I played with her; it was real and the cuffs were a symbol of that.

Lifting her hands by the link between them, I said, "Up."

She lifted her arms over her head; as they moved upward, I slid my hands down her arms before stepping back to the switch that operated the suspension cable. I lowered it down enough to hook the cuffs in the carabiner on the end.

Returning to the dresser, I pulled out the stretcher bar then attached it to her ankles. It would ensure her legs stayed spread about two feet apart until I took it off. I took a moment to drink her in, completely at my mercy. Her lips were parted as she sucked in air. She was exactly how I wanted her. Anticipation thrummed through her making her excited and nervous.

There was a small fridge hidden in the cabinetry and I removed a tray I'd called and had prepared for me earlier. I set it on the top of the dresser so it was close at hand.

Popping one of the ice cubes from a small bowl into my mouth, I took another in my hand. I made sure to let my feet fall heavily upon the ground as I walked a full circle around Alix so she would know where I was and that I'd stopped behind her. A tremor ran up her back and I could see her muscles tense under her smooth skin.

I pushed the ice cube in my mouth, holding it between my teeth then dipped my head to press it against her neck. She shivered, but didn't make any other movement as I followed her spine all the way down, leaving a cold trail of water behind. Once I hit the waistband of her panties, I stood again.

Dropping the ice cube in one hand to the other, I reached around her body and splayed my cold fingers against her stomach. She gasped and dropped her head back as I drew her to my chest. I could still feel how cold the water lining her spine was. It turned me to feel all of her skin covered with goosebumps.

Once again using the ice cube in my mouth, I caressed the sensitive skin behind her ear. Releasing the ice cube from my other hand, I pressed my ice-cold fingers between her thighs to tease her hot pussy. My fingertips slipped between her damp lips, enough to tease, but not enter her.

Even as she whimpered from the cold, she tilted her head to give me better access to her neck. The ice cube in my mouth was melted enough that I swallowed it; my fingers had heated rapidly from how hot she was.

Returning to my tray, I picked up a glass toy that had been in the freezer and put another ice cube in my mouth. I stood in front of her before lowering my lips to hers. For a short time, I let our tongues swirl around each other, the ice cube gliding from my mouth to hers and back again. When the ice cube was nearly melted, I left it behind and dipped my head to suck on her puckered nipple.

She moaned loudly and swayed on her feet. Shifting closer, I pressed the frozen toy between her thighs to let it tease her as I moved to her other nipple. I was careful to only let the toy touch her pussy lips until she was writhing against me. Finding her clit, I pressed the toy against it and she cried out in surprise.

I released her nipple and lowered myself to my knees as I smiled. Her reaction to the temperature play was better than I anticipated. Using the tip of the toy, I parted her damp folds and slid it into her. My cock throbbed from the sight of the toy pulling out wet with her arousal before disappearing once again into her. So far I had managed to ignore his pleas and demands, but the more I played with Alix, the harder it was to deny.

It was fascinating to watch as she shivered from the cold, but was no less turned on from it. When she started to buck against the toy, I couldn't stop from pressing my face between her thighs. I sucked her clit into my mouth and clicked my tongue over it as I continued thrusting the toy into her.

My cock hurt it was so hard and I was tempted to take it into my free hand, but I resisted the urge. I could wait. Instead, I used two fingers to swipe through the gathering fluids to move them back to her tightly puckered hole.

Rotating my fingers around the clenched opening, she slowly relaxed against my touch and I was able to push one finger into her. She released a loud hiss, but continued to buck against the toy and my face so I knew she was enjoying it. After a few thrusts of my finger, a second one joined in, fucking her at the same pace as the toy. She was gasping for air and moaning as she clenched down on my fingers and the toy.

She was on the verge of coming and I couldn't stop from tasting her.

"Please, Master, I need to come," she cried out. My cock jumped in appreciation for her asking me to allow her to get off.

After one final flick and slide, I forced myself to be strong and release her. Pulling my fingers and the toy from her, I sat back on my heels for a moment. I needed to gather my strength not to give into her, not yet.

Standing, I forced myself to step back from her. She was still flushed from nearly coming. Her harsh breathing made her breasts rise and fall temptingly.

"Give me a moment, Precious." I hastily exited into my private room and into the bathroom there. Washing my hands, I left the toy on the counter to be dealt with later. I stared at myself in the mirror. I'd never had someone so easily push my control. It was unnerving, but I managed to get it back. Slapping my cock, I told it to behave before returning to where she was.

Returning to the room, I smiled seeing Alix cuffed, blindfolded and spread just for me. I grabbed a candle and lighter off the dresser before stepping in front of her again.

"Something new. You still okay? Remember you can tell me to stop at any time," I said lighting the candle. She tilted her head at the sound of the lighter, probably wondering what the noise was.

"Yes, sir," she said after a moment.

"This will be hot, but I promise, it will not burn you." I pushed her hair over her shoulder to ensure it was out of the way before tilting the candle over her chest. It was a candle specially made for wax play. It melted at a lower temperature than most candles so it would not be as hot on the skin. Not that it still wouldn't redden the skin and make it draw blood to the surface.

I watched as a droplet formed before falling from the candle to land on her nipple. Instantly it cooled, but Alix gasped, telling me she felt it exactly like I wanted her to. The candle pooled and I let it drip onto her other nipple.

Alix moaned and arched her back.

It appeared that she indeed liked the wax. I moved the candle, letting it randomly leave spots all along her chest and breasts. Since it was her first time, I didn't want to do too much so I blew out the candle and set it back on the dresser. Picking up a small blade, I removed Alix's blindfold and showed her the knife.

"Don't. Move." I made sure to emphasize the words and she nodded sharply. Her breathing increased to shallow pants, but she didn't struggle or make any move to get away when I lowered it to the first splotch on her skin.

Carefully, I scraped each of the cooled wax droplets from her before meeting her eyes.

"You okay?"

"Yes, sir," she whispered, clearly nervous. It was the easiest way to remove the cooled wax since I hadn't oiled her up before hand. While I wasn't big on blades, it was also fun to play with them to add a bit of edge to scenes as long as I didn't draw blood. Blood was a hard limit for me. I didn't like *hurting* subs. I simply liked to cause pain, which was different than leaving scars and drawing blood.

A slow, lazy smile slid onto her face and I realized she'd floated into subspace. It made a spark of pride go off inside of me. Clearly our kinks lined up more than we both realized. I loved playing with wax and so did she since she had experienced it.

Reaching up, I unhooked her arms and wrapped my own around her waist to support her. Automatically her arms lowered around my neck as she rested her head against my chest. I wish I'd thought to remove the spreader bar so I could press her against the wall next to me and take her, but I hadn't so I moved her to the bed. She wasn't steady enough on her feet to fuck any other way. Laying her on her back, I stood next to the bed and forced her legs straight in the air before lining my cock up to her opening.

In one hard thrust, I was all the way in her with my balls slapping her ass. I was tempted to take her puckered hole again, but I didn't want to stop to find lube so I pounded into her already wet and tight pussy. Holding onto her thighs, I showed no mercy in slamming into her as hard as I could. The sound of my skin slapping against hers as she moaned and writhed under me only made me more turned on. It sounded like I was giving her a spanking, and that was fucking sexy.

"I want you to come, Precious," I demanded, digging my fingers into her skin. I loved seeing the little bruises my fingers left on her skin days later.

"Yes, Master," she gasped, lifting her hips into my thrusts. She'd automatically lifted her hands over her head even though I hadn't told her to. The fact she knew I liked to restrain her hands and she did it on her own to please me turned me on like mad. Dropping one of my hands between her thighs, I circled her clit. She cried out and bucked hard against me once, twice before I felt a strong surge of liquid come from her. It trickled down my balls and my own release nearly followed, but I pulled from her. Letting her legs fall over the side of the bed, I grabbed the back of her neck and forced her to sit up.

"Suck. Now," I demanded, lost to my own pleasure. All control was gone when she didn't hesitate to take me into her mouth, sucking me all the way to the back of her throat. It only took a few thrusts into her talented mouth before I yanked out with a popping sound. Using my hand, I roughly yanked on my dick before come spurted out the tip to spill over her breasts.

I wrapped a hand around her arm and made her stand before rubbing my release into her skin.

"Mine." It was more of a growl than actual speech.

"Yours, Sir." She didn't have to think about her response, it came automatically.

Chapter 9

Alix

After playing the night before, John had helped me dress before taking me home, leaving me with a soft kiss and asking me to come by his work the next day so he could take me out to lunch. I was glad when I'd gone shopping for my dress for our date I'd bought a few new outfits. I would need to add to my wardrobe if he was going to keep taking me out. I refused to wear the stuffy clothes I wore to work, and those were mostly what I owned.

Since it was a lunch date, though, I put on a skirt with a button-down shirt so I'd fit in with all the other people out for lunch in the middle of their work day. It was my day off, but I didn't want to embarrass him. I left my hair loose since he liked it that way. It took over an hour to apply my makeup since it wasn't something I normally did. It took a few attempts before I was happy with the results.

I'd never been to his office so I wasn't sure what to expect, which had butterflies battering my stomach. Leaving early so I could make sure I made it there on time, I was surprised to find he hadn't been kidding about his office being practically next door to my work. It was only a few doors down and it stated his name on the door along with a list of degrees he apparently had. I was impressed.

We didn't talk a lot about the specifics of his job, so I was a bit surprised to see "Individual and Couples Intimate Counselor" under the list of degrees. Standing outside staring at the door, I found I wasn't really surprised when I started to piece together what he'd mentioned, not to mention how good in bed he was. Finally, I knew I had to enter so I drew a deep breath and pushed open the door.

The lobby was completely empty except for a stunning blonde sitting behind a reception desk. She smiled at me as I approached her. I knew I didn't even compare to how beautiful she was and the fact John had never mentioned her appearance made me a bit upset. Deep down, I knew it was just my jealousy speaking and I tried to cleared my throat — and head — before taking the final steps to bring me right in front of her.

"I'm here for John O'Roarke," I told her as normally as I could.

"Aren't we all?" she laughed, but I didn't find her funny so I stared at her. "He's running a few minutes late with his appointment now, but I don't have him down for another appointment for a while. Are you early?"

"I don't have an appointment. I don't think anyway," I rubbed my arm self consciously.

"What's your name?" she sighed as if I was bothering her by not being on her carefully written schedule book.

"Alix Hesse," I said softly.

The woman's eyes ran over me from head to toe, slowly, assessing me while she pursed her lips.

"Let me see what I can find," she said before typing something into her computer. After a moment, she looked at me again. "I'm sorry, I can find no appointment on file for you so you must be mistaken."

"Oh. Uh, okay. Can you let him know I'm here at least?" I wasn't sure how to handle the hostile glare the woman gave me so I stepped back. There was none of the friendliness I had been initially greeted with.

"No, I can't let him know you're here. He is with a client right now and I'm not to interrupt for any reason," she sneered at me.

I was about to turn and walk out, thinking I had to be in the wrong place, when one of the doors behind the nasty woman opened and a man walked out, followed by John. As soon as he saw me, his face lit up and he held up a finger to me before speaking to the man in hushed tones. The man looked from me to the blonde.

"Are you in line?" he asked. I shook my head and gave him room.

John went back into what I assumed to be his office, only to return a moment later. He stood quietly next to the blonde until the man had exited.

"Mariah, I'm going to lunch. I'll have my phone if you absolutely need me, but I'll be back by my next appointment," John told the blonde. His eyes were on me though.

"Yes, sir," she answered him, making my eyes jump to her. Did she know about his lifestyle outside of work? Or was it simply manners that had her using that term?

John stepped close to me before placing a kiss on my lips.

"Let's go, Precious," he whispered before threading his fingers with mine.

I fought the temptation to look back at the blonde, but John was quick to move me out the door. Before the door could even shut, he had me in his arms again, his tongue pressing into my mouth.

"God, I missed you," he breathed when he pulled back a moment later.

"Mmm, maybe I need to visit you at work more often if I get greeted like that," I laughed, trying not to think of the way his secretary had treated me.

"I think I could handle that," he said, running his fingers over my cheek. Finally he stepped back and reached for my hand again. "Let's get some food. I'm starved."

After a few minutes of walking in silence, I couldn't hold it back anymore and tried to casually ask the question that I'd wanted to ask from the moment I saw him.

"So, who is your secretary?"

"Mariah. Why?" He looked down at me for a moment.

"She, uh, didn't seem to know I was coming and wasn't exactly the most friendly about letting me know I wasn't expected." I tried to shrug as if it was nothing big even though it really was.

"Really? Well, I'll be sure to let her know that is not the way to treat my girlfriend," he said.

The word "girlfriend" made me stop without meaning to.

"What? You don't want to be called my girlfriend?" He knew immediately what it was that had bothered me.

"No, I mean, I don't know. I guess I didn't realize that's what we were." What I thought we were, I didn't know either, but girlfriend and boyfriend seemed so childish compared to what we had.

"Would you prefer I say you are my sub?" he tried again.

"No. I mean… I guess girlfriend is okay. I hadn't thought about it." While I didn't mind being his submissive, I didn't think it'd be appropriate for him to go around introducing me that way.

His eyes burned into mine and I had the distinct feeling he wanted to say more on the topic, but he turned and continued down the sidewalk until we came to a little café I'd eaten at many times before.

Unable to put my jealous side to rest, I brought up the beautiful blonde again.

"So, how long has Mariah worked for you?" I asked after we'd ordered.

"About a week, I guess." He shrugged nonchalantly.

"She seems awfully comfortable for only working there for a week," I mused quietly. I didn't like being jealous, but I couldn't help it. I didn't want to lose John to some bimbo who worked for him.

"She has a lot of experience as a secretary," he said before running a hand over his face. Finally, he let out a sigh. "Plus, she's my ex so she knows what type of business I do."

I clenched my hands in my lap at his words. I tried to think how best to respond to such a revelation. It explained her hostile attitude, at least.

"Precious, don't look like that. She is an ex. Over and done with. She knows there is no chance of us getting back together. I just needed someone in a crunch and she was the only qualified applicant." John moved his chair around the table so he sat next to me. He pried my fingers apart so he could hold my hand. "She has nothing on you. You are who I want. Not her."

I nodded, but I was still trying to comprehend that he'd had his ex-lover working for him for a week and hadn't said anything to me about it. I couldn't help but feel like he was trying to hide it from me.

"Don't," he whispered, squeezing my hand. "Don't let her come between us. She's no one."

"Why didn't you tell me?" I finally managed to ask.

"I didn't think it was important. I mean it when I say she is nothing to me. She's an employee, nothing more.

Trust me, I'm not that man. I wouldn't hire her if I thought there was anything there."

There he went asking me to trust him again. Normally I did, but I had a harder time when it came to a beautiful woman whom he'd already been with. All I could do was put my faith in him. He hadn't hurt me yet — not in any way I hadn't liked — and I'd have to hope this wouldn't be the time he did.

"I trust you, John. It's just a surprise, that's all," I managed to say around the lump in my throat.

"Good. What I had with her doesn't even come close to what we have together." His thumb brushed over my knuckles.

"How long were you together?" I couldn't look at him when I asked the question.

He sighed and shifted in his seat. "A while."

"Tell me," I demanded.

"Two years."

I fought to hold back the gasp that wanted to escape. He'd been with her for longer than I'd ever been with any man. You don't stay with someone that long if you don't have a deep connection, something you think can possibly be your forever.

Our food arrived breaking the awkward moment. We both ate in silence and it wasn't one of our normal comfortable ones, but awkward, like we both had more to say but refused to bring up something that could turn into an unpleasant conversation. I had many more questions, but didn't want to keep asking since every time he answered one, it only felt like an arrow to my heart.

When we'd both given up on eating the food we'd ordered, I walked with him back to his office. He gave me a kiss on the cheek before going back to his ex and I returned home.

I'm sorry for ruining lunch. I meant to tell you about Mariah, it just never came up. Please let me come over tonight and make it up to you.

John texted me as soon as I walked through the door. I stared at the message for a long time before replying I'd be home all night. I knew I'd most likely run into his past at some point, but I didn't think it'd be a gorgeous blonde sitting in his office when I did.

I tried to watch some of the shows I'd recorded while I waited for him, but nothing held my attention. I'd already done all my household chores the day before so I found myself Googling various terms that had to do with the BDSM community to help prepare myself for anything else John might pull out of his bag of tricks.

The ice cubes and wax play the night before had been more than exciting. In fact, I looked forward to the next time he did either.

By the time he showed up on my doorstep, I had managed to get myself hot and bothered. I knew we had to talk more about his ex, but I hoped to put off the conversation as long as I could.

I opened the door wearing only a pair of panties and a bra.

"Welcome, Master." I pulled the door open far enough for him to come in while dropping my chin to my chest out of respect. Before I'd done it though, I'd seen the flash in his eyes as he shifted from John to Dom.

"Mmm, I think my little one is feeling needy," John said in his firm Dom voice as he entered. "Shut the door and come here, Precious."

I did as he instructed and followed him to where he sat on the couch. He grabbed my hips and forced me to lie over his lap.

"You are going to get a spanking for doubting me this afternoon, and then I'm going to fuck you raw to remind you once again who owns you and who you belong to. While you obviously don't realize it, as much as I own you, you own me. I am yours, more than you will ever be mine." He finished his speech by landing his open palm against my ass. The slaps rained down on opposite sides and even onto the tops of my thighs until I lost count. When he stopped the burn through my backside was fierce and tears rolled down from my eyes, but I was wet for him. I wanted to beg him to take me, but what I wanted most of all was for him to have his way with me, show me how much he wanted me and to be mine.

Pushing me off his lap, I heard the tinkling sound of his belt before his weight pushed my body into the couch and he was entering me from behind while shoving my face into the cushion. His hand fisted in my hair, yanking my head to the side.

"I need to see your face while I fuck you. I need your beauty to own my soul while I give you all my broken pieces and pray you can put them back together," he grunted as he thrust repeatedly into me.

I could only gasp in response as his cock rubbed against my g-spot, throwing me rapidly toward release. My skin burned from the friction of his pants rubbing against my ass, telling me he'd simply taken out his cock, not stripped completely. I couldn't care less. Having him on me, over me, in me, dominating me was exactly what I needed to pull my scattered thoughts to where they should've been all along.

He'd never hinted he wanted anything but what we had, as crazy and messed up as it could be. Why I had questioned it over a little bitchiness from his ex, I couldn't remember as he pounded into me.

Suddenly, he pulled from me and picked me up in his arms. He carried me to my room before putting me on the bed, face up. Grabbing a bottle of lube from my nightstand, he slicked himself up before drizzling a few drops down my slit. When his fingers started massaging my rear, I understood what he had planned.

After slipping one finger in my tightly clenched hole, he withdrew and lined up his cock. Without the normal care and patience he showed, he plunged into me.

I cried out as pain and pleasure mixed together and he cradled my bottom in his palms.

"I have to claim you again. I need the reminder that you belong to me and aren't going anywhere," he grunted. His hands clutched the sheets on either side of me instead of my hips like he normally did. I didn't like it, so I grabbed his wrists and gently pulled until he released his grip. Moving them to my hips, I smiled up at him briefly before he started rocking against me.

Something in him relaxed when I moved his hands and he slowed his frenzied movements to a more leisurely pace. I arched against him and felt my release building from the easier strokes.

When I cried out with my orgasm pinging through every nerve in my body, he collapsed on me and stopped moving. He hadn't gotten off, that much I was sure of even in my relaxed haze.

Pushing on one of his shoulders, I got him to roll onto his back where I straddled him and took him into my body again. My palms spread over his chest as I rode him slowly. His eyes latched onto mine and refused to release me.

"Yeah, Precious, ride me. Use me to give yourself pleasure," he murmured after a few minutes of no sound but that of our bodies sliding against each other.

I continued moving at the same pace I had been. It was quick enough to gradually be leading me toward another release, but not fast enough to be rushing it. I liked having a tiny bit of power over him, even if it was for a brief period of time. I wanted to show him I wasn't looking for fast and easy, but long and good. It's what I wanted not just in bed, but in our whole relationship.

It touched me that he was as upset by everything; however, it'd take more than a bitchy ex to get me to let him go. I needed him too much. I'd come to rely upon him too much to give up so easily.

When I arched my back and cried out with my release, he gripped my hips, holding me down on him as he bucked against me, letting out a guttural groan as I felt his cock throbbing deep in me as he, too, found his release.

Chapter 10

John

I hated that Mariah had ruined our date and she didn't even realize it — she was all smiles and professionalism when I returned to the office after lunch. I only half-listened to my patients for the rest of the day as I couldn't get Alix out of my head, even more so than normal. I had to find a way to make up for it. I didn't want her thinking she was anything less than what I wanted. I only wanted her, no one else. When I finally was done working for the day, all I could think about was getting to her to make sure she understood she was mine.

It was only after I roughly fucked her that I found I relaxed. Being inside her body, reinstating my ownership was the only way I could finally start to let the afternoon go. Cradling her to my chest, I rearranged us in a more comfortable position against the pillows and I ran my hand over her hair for a few minutes while I tried to center myself and regain the control I'd been barely able to hold onto since lunch.

Once I felt her relax against me and I figured she'd dozed off, I carefully escaped her grip on me to go to the bathroom. I wet a washcloth with warm water and returned to her. Taking my time, I cleaned between her thighs and crack thoroughly while making sure I didn't hurt her. She simply moaned quietly at my touch, but did nothing to stop or question me.

I left the washcloth on the counter before washing my flaccid dick in the sink, then went back to the bed. Pulling her close, I soothed one hand down her back and held her hips close with the other. It didn't matter that the arm I'd snaked under her was losing circulation; I needed her in my arms and to be touching her as much as I could, even if she was sleeping.

Time passed while I watched her sleep — it could've been minutes or hours, I couldn't tell or care. At some point, she opened her eyes and looked up at me with a lazy smile.

"Why aren't you sleeping? You have to be exhausted after working all day and dealing with my hysterics, then fucking me senseless," she murmured sleepily. Her palm ran up my chest, then down my arm before making its way back to where I'd had it trapped against me.

"I don't want to miss a moment with you," I breathed.

"You are crazy. Sleep now so you aren't tired tomorrow." She pulled back and I released her. Rolling to her side, she put her back to me before scooting into me again. "Sorry, I normally sleep on this side."

"It's okay. I can still hold you like this," I said, folding one arm under my pillow as the other slid around her waist. I shoved a leg between hers and breathed in her scent.

"Please sleep. I'll feel terrible tomorrow knowing that it was my fault you didn't rest," she pleaded.

"I'll be fine. Go back to sleep," I whispered.

She did as I instructed and before long I felt my eyes getting heavy, finally giving in. As much as I didn't want to miss a moment, sometimes the body took over.

In the morning, I woke to a soft caress running along my abdomen and peeked open one eye. Alix was smiling at me as she sat on the bed, already showered and dressed.

"Wake up, Master. You need to go to work, sir," she said softly, but hearing her use such words outside of the club and any sexual activity woke me up faster than anything else.

"Keep talking to me like that and I'll be late to work." I rolled onto my back and stretched.

"Nope. Not today. You were late because of me once already and I refuse to be the cause of it again." She patted my stomach and stood up from the bed. "Plus, I have stuff to do so you have to leave."

"Am I being kicked out of your house?" I gaped at her. I'd never had someone do such a thing.

"Mmm, as tempting as it would be…." She rubbed her chin as if she was considering it. "I can also give you a key so you can lock up after you leave."

"A key?" My heart stuttered a beat before racing. A key to her place? Was she really ready to take that step with me?

"That you can use for now," she clarified, and my heart slowed.

"I suppose I'll hurry and get ready so you don't have to worry about leaving me with a key." I tried to not let my disappointment show. I knew things were moving rapidly between us, but it was like so much had already been established and shared between us that other couples didn't get to until they'd been dating for months or even years.

"Oh, stop it. If you want a key, just say so. I have no problem giving you one. I figured you'd freak out if I gave you one on my own," she said with a shrug before looking away.

"Would you like a key to my place? I'll get one made for you today," I said hoping to show her I was more than ready.

"I don't even know where you live, so it really wouldn't do me any good," she sighed, and I realized what an ass I'd been. I'd never taken her to my place, so of course she was a bit hesitant to give me a key to hers.

"Well, I guess that'll have to be remedied then, won't it?" I climbed from the bed and took her into my arms. "I feel the connection too. It's quick, but who cares. As long as we're both on the same page and feeling the same things, then fuck everyone else and what they expect or say."

She nodded her head, but refused to meet my eyes. Hooking a finger under her chin, I forced her to lift her head.

"Don't do that. Talk to me. Tell me what is going on in that head of yours."

"I've never been good at relationships, I don't know how to do them or how to keep you happy once the newness wears off." She lifted a shoulder as a sad half-smile tilted her lips.

"Just you being you makes me happy. Forget about everything else, because it'll come naturally." I pressed a soft kiss to her lips, then another on her forehead. "I do need to go, though. Will I see you tonight?"

"I don't know when I'll get off work and I have a lot going on right now, so probably not. Tomorrow?"

I could see the plea in her eyes so I smiled.

"Yes, tomorrow then. I'll text you later," I said before pulling on my clothes and leaving. It was getting harder and harder to leave her when I had to go to work, but I had no other choice. At least my day was filled with out-of-the-office appointments, which would be good to keep me distracted.

Returning to my apartment to shower and change, I realized I needed to either start taking a change of clothes with me, leave clothes at Alix's or bring her to my place so I wouldn't have to always make an extra stop before going to work.

Since I only had to stop in briefly, then head out to meet clients, thankfully I wasn't late to meet them. I'd only talked briefly with Mariah to get my schedule for the day before leaving again. She'd frowned at my brisk demeanor, but I didn't have time to spare.

My first couple was a pair I hadn't met before outside of the office, Tara and Chase. They hadn't been together long, but were already feeling the strain of hidden desires. I knew Tara from when she'd been in another relationship. She had a hard time simply expressing what she wanted without me there because of her past. I was working to get her to open up and not fear every man would be like the one who'd made her so afraid to share herself.

We were meeting at Tara's because it was where she was most comfortable. When I arrived, they were both waiting on the couch for me in jeans. My suits often made me feel overdressed, but also in control. I wasn't the one getting intimate, they were, so they were the ones who needed to be comfortable.

"Welcome, John." Tara smiled and shook my hand.

"Tara. Chase." I nodded at each of them as she closed the door behind me. "Since I've already met with Tara about today, I'd like to have her go prepare while Chase and I chat for a few minutes."

"Okay," Tara said eagerly before sauntering down the hall. If I didn't know what she'd been through I'd think she was simply enjoying the voyeurism of having someone watching them, but there was a lot more under the surface when it came to her.

"How are you feeling, Chase?" I asked sitting next to him.

"Anxious. I've never done anything like this and I'm afraid I won't be able to, uh, perform." He looked down at his hands as he picked at his nails.

"You'll forget I'm even there after a bit, I promise. Now I know we've talked about a lot of topics in my office, but today I want to specifically address spanking and restraining, as that is what Tara requested we start with." I crossed one ankle over the opposite knee and leaned back against the cushion.

"I've never done either. I suppose you could say I'm all vanilla," he laughed softly, but I simply nodded. I knew he was, but that was easily changed when done in small amounts and as long as he was comfortable and open minded.

"I'll be there to guide and teach you. Don't be afraid to speak up if you are uncertain or uncomfortable with anything. Now, how about we go see what Tara has prepared for you?" I stood and he followed after, swallowing hard. He led me toward the bedroom even though I knew where it was, but he didn't know I'd been in her house before with her ex and I wasn't about to tell him.

He stopped in front of the door that was left slightly cracked and wiped his hands on his thighs before pushing it open farther. A breath hissed out from between his teeth at the sight that awaited us.

Tara was leaning over the foot of the bed, naked, her ass pushed into the air. There were scarves piled to one side of her and a riding crop on the other. Her body was already flushed and her folds glistened with her arousal.

"If I wasn't here, where would you start?" I whispered to Chase. He cleared his throat and shifted uncomfortably.

"I'd bang her just like that," Chase said, shyly.

"No, that's not how it's going to happen. Strip to your boxers," I instructed and stepped back from him to give him a bit of privacy to do so. He hesitated for a moment before finally pulling off his shirt and shucking his jeans. "Go stand on the side of the bed and I'll show you how to restrain her like this."

He nodded and moved to stand next to her.

"No, next to the bed, not her." I stepped behind her. "If you are going to touch her, it's to show her who is in control, not to arouse her."

Running my hand up the center of her back firmly, I snagged a handful of her hair and pulled her head up off the bed. A gasp left her, but she wiggled her hips against me.

"Do not move or I will be forced to punish you," I growled at Tara, who whimpered but nodded. I turned to look at Chase. "Like that."

"Uh, okay," he stuttered.

"Now, take one of the scarves and wrap it around her wrist then pull it back to wrap it around. Knot it around her ankle. It'll spread her wide and make it hard for her to wiggle around much, which is what we want," I instructed and watched as he attempted to do as I asked. Surprisingly, he did it quite well. "Repeat it on the other side now."

The position made her spread her legs wide to the sides of her full mattress while holding her torso flat against the bed so her wrists could almost touch her ankles. If the scarves had been shorter, we'd have to find a different way, but I'd known they'd be long enough.

"Behind her. Touch her as you move so she knows where you are, unless you want to surprise her. That's a benefit of this position. You can do as you please and she is at your mercy. Remember, though, this is about trust. She is trusting you not to take it further than she wants, and you are trusting her to let you know when she's had enough." I moved beside him and lifted his hand to her ass. "Caress, squeeze, her flesh. It'll start the increased blood flow she desires. Make her want you, want more of what you can give her, what she can't get from anyone but you."

After a few moments, I could tell he was getting the hang of it. He used both his hands on her bottom and she thrashed on the bed, moaning out her desire for more.

"Now." I nodded once at him and he knew instantly what I meant as he lifted one hand and brought it down against her ass. She groaned and yelled for more. He repeated the move, but harder, on the other side.

"Yes!" she screamed out. "Harder!"

I stepped back as Chase took over and took turns slapping one side then the other. When her skin was bright pink, I returned to his side.

"Since you have her blood flowing well to that area, you may want to caress her skin between blows since it can get a lot more intense as the skin becomes a deeper hue of pink and red. Listen to her and she'll tell you what she needs." I walked around to his other side and picked up the riding crop. It was short and black with a leather flap at the end. "When your hand grows tired or too sore, you can use the crop to continue, but it'll sting a lot more than your hand will, so keep that in mind. Or you can use it to tease her."

"How would you tease with that?" Chase asked, halting his movements to watch me.

"May I?" I asked, showing him I wanted to stand where he was. He nodded and stepped aside. I trailed the tip of the leather down her spine from her nape to the top of her ass. "You can use the tip to stimulate, like this.

"Or you can use it to sensitize other areas, like this." I gently slapped the outside of her thighs a few times before moving to the insides. "And when you feel comfortable, you can even use it to bring an orgasm if she's turned on enough."

I slapped the crop against her wet lips and she arched her back as much as she could as she gasped.

"Would you like more, Tara?" I asked, wanting him to see exactly how turned on she was.

"Yes, please," she begged beautifully.

Again, I brought the crop to her sensitive skin. Her body was shuddering and I wanted to bring her to climax, but it wasn't my job. He'd have to take that pleasure. It was simply knowing how easily she handed over the control and blossomed beautifully under the crop. It reminded me of Alix when I'd used a crop on her.

"Of course, if you don't want to let her get off easily, you can simply drag the tip through her lips and tease her. Then you can use the handle to fill her anally or vaginally. The possibilities are as endless or as limited as your mind makes them. Try new things, with her consent of course. And always make sure you wash your toys afterwards." I handed Chase the crop and stepped back to the corner to let him have a hand at teasing and tormenting her. He seemed most fascinated with slapping against her pussy, since that got the most vocal responses from her, and she was coming all over the toy after only a few hits.

"Now you can either take her like this, keep playing with her until you are happy with the number of times she's come, or you can release her and take things in another direction. It's all up to how you want things to go or where you thinks he wants them to go," I said loudly from across the room. I leaned against the wall and stuffed my hands in my pockets to watch as they moved on to fucking and coming. I helped him untie her when he was done, then after a swift good bye to the cuddling couple, I left.

Another happy couple. Time to move on to another pair who was in need of assistance.

The rest of the day was spent with similar clients, most of whom had fairly normal requests when it came to my assistance. It was always about the fear of rejection, the fear of not being accepted for their desire of something "different" or "weird". All it usually took was a conversation with both parties and they'd normally agree to give it a try. If an idea was flat-out denied, we would try something else more tame and work our way back to the idea at another time.

When I finally returned to the office, I found Mariah waiting with her patented smile and a stack of notes for me. I was still getting used to the idea that calls weren't being forwarded directly to my cell for me to handle, but to her. It was a nice break not to be constantly interrupted; however, I had always put my phone on silent while with clients so as to not break the scene or moment for them.

Sitting behind my desk, I started going through the slips she'd given me. After a few minutes, she knocked and entered my office. I looked up expectantly.

"I'm going to head out, but wanted to make sure you had everything you needed." She leaned against the wall.

"No, I think I'll be fine," I said before returning to the notes. When I didn't hear the door shut, I lifted my head again to find her still watching me. "Anything else?"

She strutted closer to me, resting a hip on the corner near my hand.

"Can you read my handwriting on those? I know it's so sloppy sometimes." She bent closer like she was peering at the papers. What she was really doing was giving me a glance down her shirt whether she intended to or not. I'd seen it before and wasn't the least bit interested.

"They're fine," I said, briskly.

"Okay, good," she breathed before pushing off my desk. She walked back to the door before swinging her head around, making her long hair go flying. "You know, I was thinking of going to get a drink at the bar next door. You want to go with?"

"No, I don't drink. You know that." I shook my head while keeping my eyes down.

"Well, if you change your mind, I'll be there for a while," she said, finally leaving my office.

I waved my hand in front of my face a few times. Her perfume was over-powering when she got too close to me. I'd never noticed it before but the last few days it'd been annoying me. If it kept up I'd have to ask her to tone it down. It couldn't be only me who was bothered by it.

Throughout the day I'd texted Alix a few short messages between clients, but I missed her more than ever. I'd been spoiled seeing her so much the past few days. Thankfully most of the notes were things I could put off until the next day when I'd be in the office, so I gathered my belongings and locked up. Walking to the hotel, I straightened my tie and ran a hand through my hair before walking into the hotel lobby.

I spotted Alix and smiled as she chatted with Jennifer behind the counter. Locking my eyes on her face, I headed toward her. Unfortunately, I was stopped when I heard my name being called. I turned to find Mariah walking out of the bar area toward me. Frowning, I stepped closer to her.

"Yes?" I asked through gritted teeth. I didn't like when anyone came between me and Alix and that's exactly what she was doing by making me wait even longer until I could have my woman wrapped in my arms.

"I just… um…" She trailed off, looking over my shoulder for a moment before meeting my gaze again. "I thought you had changed your mind about a drink."

"No, you were mistaken." I started to move away again, but her hand on my forearm stopped me.

"Sorry, I didn't mean to interrupt your night," she said, bowing her head. I looked at her demure posture and had a flashback to one of the many times we'd played together. She'd been a perfect sub, always so easy to dominate and eager to please.

"It's fine." I nodded once before turning away from her. Instantly, I found Alix's eyes on me. She'd seen the exchange and was watching me with confusion in her eyes. Closing the distance between us, I smiled at Jennifer before turning my attention back to Alix. "Can I speak to you?"

"Of course," Alix answered before moving around from behind the counter and holding out her hand in the direction of her office. I followed behind her and closed the door once we were both inside.

"She had asked me to join her for a drink and I declined. When she saw me here, she thought I'd changed my mind. I don't think she knew you work here," I explained before she could say anything.

"Okay," she said.

I stepped close to her and pulled her into my arms and kissed her forehead gently.

"There is nothing there," I spoke softly.

"I know. It's still hard for me to know you work with your ex," she said, finally breaking her silence.

"Don't let it get under your skin. She doesn't matter to me as anything other than the respite she gives me from constant phone calls and scheduling." I ran my hand over her hair, breathing her scent in.

She nodded against my shirt, holding me around the waist. After a moment, she pulled back.

"You have to go. I have a client I'm expecting any moment. That's actually why I was up there with Jennifer. Waiting where I'd be easier to find since I've never met them before." She pushed closer to seal her lips against mine for a chaste kiss. "I'll call you when I get off."

"Please do," I sighed, not wanting to let go of her. I kissed her once more then exited her office. By going straight to the elevator, I avoided another run-in with Mariah.

I had a few hours of being on call for the online counseling so I'd be stuck in my home office for the rest of the night anyway.

Chapter 11

Alix

After getting off work, I drove home and called John. We talked on the phone for over an hour before I admitted to exhaustion. He invited me over to his place for dinner the next night and I was excited to finally see where he lived. In fact, thoughts of him kept me up long after our call was over. Not all of them good, either. Although he swore there was nothing between him and his secretary, it was hard to miss the fact that he smelled of her perfume. Not to mention the little scene in the hotel lobby.

She'd touched him and acted the part of a submissive when he'd reprimanded her about whatever it had been that they'd been talking about. Knowing how long they'd been together, I tried to brush it off as habit, but it still bothered me.

Eventually, I fell asleep as I focused on my upcoming date with John. I focused on all the other times I'd been with him had been, not the confusion and questions that surrounded his ex.

The next day I was surprised to be woken by a delivery man bearing a large bouquet of flowers from John. The card was a simple note:

Can't wait for tonight.
John

It brought a smile to my face to know he'd been thinking about me so early in the morning, or perhaps he'd ordered them after we'd talked the night before; either way they were a sweet start to the day.

Thankfully I had to work so I couldn't sit on my couch all day and focus on what John may or may not have had planned for our time together. There was an event, too, so I'd be busier than normal getting it set up.

Knowing I was going to be seeing John that evening, I put on a sheer thong to go with my garter belt and thigh highs along with a matching black bra. I put a dress I planned to change into in a bag, then put on a dress suit, my normal work clothes. Not wanting to deal with an extra pair of shoes, I put on the most comfortable pair of four-inch heels I owned and headed out.

The event went off without a hitch and I stood in the back of the room in case I was needed for anything, which was a good thing when one of the servers let me know they were running low on the champagne being served.

I went to the back where the extra stock was kept and managed to find another box of it and had one of the men help me wheel it back to the party. When I returned to my place, I spotted a familiar blonde I hadn't noticed before. It was Mariah. I wasn't sure what she was doing at my event, but since she seemed to know other people there, I wasn't going to interrupt.

"So, how are you, dear?" one of the guests was asking Mariah.

"Oh, just great. I have this really amazing boyfriend who makes me feel like a million bucks. We're keeping it on the down-low right now, though." She glanced from one side to the other and then lowered her head toward the other woman, but not her voice. "You know, he's dealing with his last girlfriend. He doesn't know how to tell her it's over since I've come into his life. She's super-clingy, always texting him when he's at work, aggravating him, bothering him when he's so busy already."

"Doesn't it bother you? Knowing your man is with another woman?" the other woman asked, surprised.

"No. I mean, I get to be with him every day and some nights. He only sees her some nights when he can't keep her at bay anymore. Trust me, when he's with me, he makes it more than clear he's just waiting for the right time to break it off with her." She let out a loud sigh. "She has to know about me. I mean, he leaves smelling like me."

"You would think…" The other woman trailed off, obviously not sure how to respond.

"Well, one day soon. He started talking about marriage, but I told him I'm not willing to even go there until he breaks it off with her," Mariah said, shaking her head.

"Good for you. Hopefully that'll make him move his feet a little faster," the other woman said, nodding.

"Well, you'd think after being together for two years before he'd know how good we are together and that'd help motivate him." She ran her hands through her hair as she shifted and lifted her eyes right to where I was. Her face flushed and she actually looked embarrassed. "Oh, Alix, how nice to see you. I didn't know you'd be here."

"I planned the event, so of course I'm here," I answered, even though I felt like fleeing from the room. I couldn't believe what I'd heard. It only confirmed the thoughts that had kept me up the night before.

"Well, you'll have to excuse me, I have to get back to work. I just wanted to stop in and say hi to a few old friends." Mariah smiled at the woman next to her before winking at me and leaving.

I spent the last part of the party with my head spinning. It felt like the world was falling apart under my feet. When I returned to my desk, I sat down and put my head in my hands, fighting tears.

When my phone rang, I jumped and sniffled before answering, trying to sound as normal as possible.

"Hello?"

"Precious? What's wrong?" It was John.

"Nothing. What are you doing?" I asked, wiping my nose with a tissue. I didn't know how to bring up the conversation I'd overheard. Who was telling the truth? Was John with Mariah and trying to find a way to break up with me? Had she been talking about another man? Why had she seemed embarrassed to find me there? It had to be John she was talking about, right? It was the only conclusion I could come up with.

"I'm between clients and needed to hear your voice," he whispered in a husky tone. "Are you going to tell me what's wrong?"

"Is Mariah seeing someone?" I blurted out the question without meaning to.

"What? I don't know. I haven't asked and I don't really care whether she is or isn't to be honest," he answered, sounding frustrated. "Now, what does that have to do with anything?"

"I needed to know," I sighed. I didn't know why I'd asked. It's not like he'd come straight out and tell me it was him if they were together behind my back.

"I wish you'd just forget she is around, baby. I'm looking for someone to replace her, okay? As soon as I find someone else, I'll get rid of her. Now let's talk about something else. I didn't call to talk about her," he groaned. "I have plans for you tonight. I'll show you how important you are and how much you mean to me."

"I can't wait," I breathed. All my emotions were at war within me. I wanted to believe him, but it was hard to understand what was going on with his ex. It was confusing and I felt like I was being yanked around. While I was shy and kept to myself most of the time, I wanted to get to the bottom of what was going on between the two of them before I called it quits. The fact that I was very likely in love with John made it that much harder to see him as a cheater and a liar, but if he was then I'd have to leave and never look back. My issues were bad enough without adding in more.

"Meet me at my office when you get off?"

"Okay," I responded and hung up the phone. I had the rest of the afternoon to get myself together.

By the time I got off, I had managed to chalk up Mariah's conversation to lies and changed into a tight black dress before heading over to John's office. When I walked in, I was grateful to find the office empty. John's door was slightly ajar and I knocked twice before pushing it further open. Lifting his head, he smiled as his eyes ran over me.

"Well, that's the sexiest thing to walk into my office all day. Hello, beautiful." John pushed back from his desk and patted his knee.

I walked over and sat on his thigh.

"I just have to write one more email and then I'll be ready to go," he said, placing one arm on either side of me as he tapped on his keyboard. It only took a moment before he turned the computer off and pulled me closer to him as he leaned back in his chair. I could feel the hard length of him against my ass. "I could bend you over my desk and fuck you right here. You are so hot in that dress."

"Wait until you see what's under it." I looked over my shoulder and wiggled an eyebrow at him.

"Tease. You're lucky I don't fuck in the office or I really would do it. If I had you on my desk I'd get hard every time I sat here and that would get really awkward," he laughed, and nuzzled his face into my neck. "Now what do you say to getting a tour of my place?"

"Let's go." I smiled and stood.

Resting a hand on my lower back, he locked up and escorted me to the hotel. It was odd being right back where I'd spent my day; then again, I wasn't an employee, but a guest this time. As we waited for the elevator, John turned me around so I was looking at my vacant office.

"You know, I used to make extra trips to and from my apartment just so I could catch a glimpse of the beautiful woman behind that desk right there," he whispered in my ear, his lips brushing against it as he spoke. "Then one day, she looked up and I knew she was doing something naughty while she watched me. Had me so fucking hard I almost came over to give you something so much better."

"But you didn't," I whined, clearly remembering the encounter he was talking about.

"I didn't. I fucking jacked off thinking about it three times that night, though." He bit down on my earlobe as he rubbed his erection against my back. "Hell, I still do sometimes."

"You masturbate?" I gasped in surprise.

"Of course," he said as the elevator dinged with it's arrival. He pulled me into the elevator by my hand and pushed the button for the top floor.

"But…" I couldn't believe he was allowed to when I wasn't.

"I don't do it obsessively. It's like the difference between a casual drinker and a drunk. I do it maybe twice a day while you did it a hell of a lot more than that, didn't you?"

I frowned and lowered my head. I didn't like the way the conversation was going. While it was arousing as hell to imagine him touching himself, I hated feeling like the odd man out once again because of the addiction that plagued me.

"No, don't." He lifted my chin with a finger. I refused to meet his eyes though. "Look at me. Now."

It was his Dom voice and I instantly looked up.

"You are perfect the way you are. There is nothing wrong with you. Think of it this way, you can drink alcohol while I can not. Everyone has something that is their weakness."

I could tell from the flash in his eyes that there was more behind what he was saying.

"You can't or won't drink?" I had always thought it was simply a choice he made.

"Won't. I refuse to." It was his turn to feel uncomfortable.

"Why?" I pressed.

He ran a hand through his hair and sighed.

"It's not a conversation I want to have in an elevator. It's not a pleasant story. I will share it with you another night. I simply want to enjoy your company tonight, not deal with such deep issues as the ones we're getting into with our pasts," he finally said as the elevator arrived at his floor.

I was curious and wanted to know more. We would have to talk about it at some point if things were to ever get further than they were between us.

"Another night, okay? Promise." He lifted my hand and placed a kiss on my knuckles before leading me to his door. Pushing it open, he let me enter first.

My mouth dropped open. I had no idea there was a place in the entire building so extravagant as his apartment.

John took the time to show me all the rooms. It wasn't huge, but everything looked expensive and fragile, not exactly the way I imagined the place he lived. By the time we returned to the living room, I didn't know what to say about the place.

"It's, uh, wow…" I trailed off with a shrug.

"I know, it's a bit over the top. It's not me, but I don't normally spend much time here. I had a designer come in and fix it up about a week ago when I realized how boring it was. I didn't want you to think I lived in a crappy shack or something," he said, smiling embarrassedly.

"It's lovely, but I don't care about all that. I care about you," I said, wrapping my arms around him.

"Mmm, I care about you too." He kissed my lips before stepping out of my embrace and pulling me by the hand toward the kitchen. "Come, I had some food put in the oven to keep it warm for us."

"Oh?" I was surprised. Apparently he had staff of some sort to help him. I knew how busy his life could get so I didn't say anything about it. He acted almost like the fact he had such a nice place to live in, with help, wasn't something he was particularly proud of.

He pulled out two plates from the oven and set them on the already prepared table before holding a handout showing me where he wanted me to sit. Walking over to the table, I sat down as he helped tuck the chair under me. He sat next to me and a wicked smiled played over his features.

"I can't wait to have you here for a party with some, er, like-minded individuals. There is something I've been planning for you and you'll enjoy it. Another night, though."

It seemed he had many plans for the future and it made my heart skip a beat to know he had no intention of letting me go any time soon. I didn't want to let go of *him* anytime soon.

After the hint of something incredibly naughty in the works, the rest of the conversation turned to mundane topics as we got to know each other more over dinner. It turned out he didn't have many people over to his place, so the fact that he wanted to have a party sounded a bit odd, but I'd do anything he asked. Anything for him. Always.

Once we'd both eaten our meals, he pushed away his plate before holding a hand down for me. Slipping my hand into his, I let him lead me down the hall toward his bedroom. My heart raced and my breathing accelerated as we drew closer. I never knew what he had planned for me and it kept me on the edge between scared and aroused.

Closing the door, he slid his hands into his pockets and spread his feet shoulder-width apart. I knew the look immediately. It was his Dom stance.

"Take off your dress, Precious."

I peeled my dress off, revealing my sheer bra and panties. A groan rumbled from him and I slowly turned in a circle for him. When I turned to face him again, I slowly dropped to my knees, spreading my legs so he could see all that I was offering to him, resting my hands on my thighs.

He stepped away and I heard an odd sound, but shortly that after a new smell came over me. It was incense of some type, and it smelled exactly like John.

"Tonight we are going to play with your senses. We have already mastered the blindfold, so I will leave that off as long as you behave, Precious." He stepped in front of me again so I could see he'd removed his shoes, but his slacks ended perfectly on top of his feet so I knew he hadn't completely stripped. "You will be able to see; however, that is all you will be able to do besides feel. I have headphones you will wear and I am going to restrain you. Do you understand?"

"Yes, sir," I murmured, feeling my body heat rise simply from his words. I'd never had my hearing restricted before so I wasn't sure how much of a difference it would make. I trusted him, though.

"Climb on the bed," he instructed, stepping back.

I pushed to my feet and without looking in his direction, I went to the bed. Centering myself, I lay on my back.

"Stomach."

I rolled onto my stomach, turning my head so I could breathe. Then I felt the bed shift as he knelt next to me. I could see from the corner of my eye that he had already removed his shirt and was dressed only in his pants. His abdominal muscles flexed and shifted as he moved both my wrists behind my back, clasping them together with a leather binding. Moving down the bed, he bent my legs and bound my ankles together as well.

His palms pressed my inner thighs apart so they were spread, revealing the most intimate parts of my body before I felt the bindings on my wrist attached to the ones on my ankles. I was efficiently restrained and at his mercy.

"Is that uncomfortable in any way?" he asked, moving back to kneel next to my chest.

"No, sir."

"Good." I felt him reach off the bed for something before his hands pulled my hair from underneath me. "Lift your head, I am going to put the headphones on now. I am also going to place a small ball in your hand — if you feel like you need to stop at any time, drop it or use your voice, but I want you to have another method since you will be quite... overwhelmed."

"Understood, sir." I didn't really, but I knew I would shortly. He pressed a ball that was about the size of a walnut into my right palm and closed my hand around it. It was small enough I could hold it but not so small I'd forget it was there, which I assumed was the point.

He slid heavy headphones over my ears before helping me rest my head back against the pillow. It was a bit awkward with the thick circle over my ear as it pressed into the soft pillow, but I found the pillow adjusted around it to still comfortably support my head.

The song playing was one with a heavy beat and futuristic sounds. It was easy to get lost in and after a moment I had nearly forgotten where I was except for the fact that my arms and legs were immobile.

Closing my eyes, I realized I may as well have been blindfolded because I had no desire to keep my eyes open. All I could see was directly next to the bed and from the shift of the mattress, John was more toward the foot. Something slowly wrapped around one leg, then the other before wrapping around each arm.

John's hand slid up my back until he could grasp my hair, and thus lift my head. My eyes opened immediately as I gasped. His face was in my view and he had a strand of pearls in his hand. It was then I knew exactly what was wrapped around me. It was pearls. He'd surrounded me with the precious stones.

Releasing my hair, he carefully threaded the strand he'd held under me to wrap it around my neck in addition to the one I already wore. Except he didn't leave it like a necklace; no, instead he trailed the two long ends down my back before I felt them being pressed between my crack.

His palm came down on one side of my ass and I clenched my cheeks together. A soft pat on the sore cheek let me know that was exactly what he'd wanted. It was getting hard to focus on what he was doing or anticipate what would be next since the music was pulsing through my ears, my blood pounding in time to it. The pearls added to the feeling of restraint from the bindings on my wrists and ankles. Then there were the pearls around my neck, just tight enough that if I clenched my cheeks hard enough, they dug into my throat.

A sharp, pricking sensation ran down the bottom of one foot from the tip of my big toe to my heel. I squirmed from it. It hurt, but not so much I couldn't handle it. When it disappeared, I expected it on the opposite foot, but the spines of the Wartenburg wheel wandered over the inside of my thigh. When I jumped again, John's hand landed on my ass sharply. I cried out. He didn't want me to move and I knew it, but couldn't help it when I had no idea where he'd move to next.

Reaching the apex of my thighs, the pricks disappeared. He wasn't pressing hard enough to pierce the skin, which I knew he could, but hard enough I knew I'd have little impressions left behind for a while.

Long moments passed without a touch of any kind and I relaxed, calming my breathing. The spines returned to my other foot and I bit down on my lip so I didn't squirm.

Each time a point pushed against my skin, I felt a pulse within my pussy answering with its own cry of need. The pain moved to my unused thigh and the higher it climbed the closer I drew to a building orgasm. I couldn't get off from it, but I could get damn close. The sharp spikes of pain made me want to writhe, made me want to beg, but I did neither.

The fun was just starting and I wanted to keep from begging as long as I possibly could. This was a test to show John I could take everything he wanted to give me. I could be all he needed. I knew it deep in my heart and I wanted to make sure he knew it as well.

John gripped the side of my panties and yanked on them. The elastic stretched, drawing them up into my slit painfully before I felt them tear under the force he exerted on them. I squirmed until I felt his chest press against my thighs and he tugged on the other side, tearing the rest of them from me. *Relief.* The damp fabric had rubbed abrasively against my tender flesh.

I jumped when I felt something cold press against my heated skin. John's fingers slid along the outside of my pussy lips, never touching where I needed him. I was glad I'd made time to get waxed earlier in the week so I knew it was as smooth as it could be for him.

His touch disappeared, only to be replaced with something else, something foreign. The item seemed to loosely cup my entire pussy at once and a moment later I knew why. It was a pump. It sucked my clit and pussy lips up into it, sensitizing them further. While I'd never experienced one before, I had done research and knew what to expect — or so I thought.

The pump's grip on me grew tighter and tighter and I moaned as it became almost too much, then it stopped. I could feel all the blood in my body rushing toward that single point, enlarging it slightly. Just when I thought the pressure was subsiding, it sucked me up again and again, pushing me toward the fine edge of pain, and then — nothing.

John ran kisses down the exposed skin between the strands of pearls on my thighs and when he reached my core, all pressure seized as he released me from the pump. Blood pounded in my clit as my arousal reached an entirely new level I'd never known before.

His lips took my clit into his mouth and flicked his tongue over it, making me whimper while clenching my hand tighter around the ball in my hand. It was the only part of my body I seemed able to control or do anything about. The only thing left to ground me from the multitude of stimulations bombarding me at once.

The air smelled strongly of the scent that always seemed to accompany John's presence. The music was dull in my ears as I concentrated on what was going on between my thighs. My eyes were closed tightly, not needing anything to distract my mind from the pleasure being rained upon me.

As quickly as his mouth had latched onto me, it was gone. In its place was the pump. I lost track of how many times he switched between his mouth and the plumping instrument. All I knew was I was incredibly sensitive and being held on the brink of an orgasm the entire time, but he always made sure to stop just short of me falling into bliss. Finally I couldn't handle any more.

"Please, sir, I can't.. I can't take any more. I'm too sensitive," I gasped, barely able to form the words through the haze in my brain.

I felt the bed shift as he moved next to me and I saw the pump being set on the table in my eyeline. Yes, he wanted me to see what he was using on me, reminding me of it even as he moved on to something else.

When the sharp points of the Wartenburg wheel returned, I screamed. He ran them over my pussy lips gently at first, but I was so tender he might as well have broken skin with them. The longer he ran them up one side then down the other, the harder he pushed on them. It was only when I feared he'd make me bleed that I dropped the ball from my hand.

I was floating and unable to make my lips form any words, except for moans. Instantly the points were gone and a cool cream was being spread over where it'd tormented me. The headphones were removed next and it was a shock to be plunged into the peacefulness of the room after such a long time hearing nothing but my own breathing, heartbeat and the same song on repeat.

"How are you doing, Precious?" John asked, running his fingers over my cheek.

I tried to respond, but I was so far into subspace I couldn't.

"Mmm, I do love the look on your face while you float," he murmured kissing my cheek. "One last thing and then you can float off to sleep."

I heard the words, but they made no sense to my numbed brain. The bed shifted as he moved between my thighs once more. There was a firm, hard pressure before I realized he was entering me.

A moan escaped me as I welcomed him. In one thrust, he was fully in me and I felt a tug on the pearls around my neck.

"Shit, you are so wet," John groaned, huskily. "I need you to come. I need to have you bathe me in your release, then I'll fill you with my come so deep you'll never be free of me."

His hips pistoned into me. Skin slapped against skin as I was jostled on the bed. My orgasm, which had been fading, ignited and started a fire in every limb of my body as it crawled through me toward the powder keg between my thighs. Closer and closer the flames moved toward the impending explosion.

"Yes, that's it, Precious. Suck me deeper. Wrap around me so tight it hurts. Fuck. Yes!" he cried out, moving even faster against me as he tightened the cord around my neck. I struggled to draw breath, but it heightened every sensation I was feeling. The pearls on my legs slid along my skin as he moved, feeling like little hands everywhere, touching me, caressing me.

When I exploded, I felt like every molecule in my body had combusted and I was no longer a living thing, but simply a rush of emotions. Higher than I'd ever been before.

I heard John grunt as he followed me over the cliff. The pressure around my windpipe released and I drew in a deep breath as I slowly returned to my body, which was still twitching from such an intense orgasm.

Slowly John removed the pearls he'd draped me in, then the bindings on my wrists and finally the ones on my ankles. He grabbed a small bottle from the nightstand I hadn't spotted before. Sitting next to me, he slowly used the oil to massage each of my extremities back to life.

"You okay?" he asked finally curling up next to me. His hand gently slid up and down my spine.

"Yes. More than fine. Sleep. Now," I grumbled not in the mood for talking. He chuckled and pulled the blankets over us.

"I can do that," he said, pulling me to his chest. "Sleep well, Precious."

I mumbled something unintelligible as I snuggled into him. As I drifted off to sleep, I heard him whisper.

"I love you, Alix. You are mine, all mine. I refuse to let you go. Ever. I can't live without you."

Chapter 12

John

The night had gone exactly as planned — I had wanted to show Alix how good we were together, so I'd spent hours pussy worshiping. There was nothing else I'd rather do than torment her and keep her right on the edge of coming. Sure, I enjoyed making her skin turn pink or even red at times, but there was nothing compared to her begging me to take her because she was so turned on. Nothing.

As I'd held her I whispered words I hadn't meant to but thankfully she'd already been asleep and didn't hear them. I wouldn't know what I'd do if she tried to leave me. I'd backed off on constantly checking on her because she was so open with me about what was going on with her since she'd found out who I was. I knew at some point I'd have to tell her how much more there was to how I'd met her, that I completely flat-out stalked her, but I wanted to put it off for as long as I could, possibly forever.

Then there was the whole issue with not telling her I'd been the online counselor who'd talked with her a few times. I knew she'd feel betrayed, like I'd peered into her private life uninvited since we hadn't really been together at that point. I was mostly thankful she hadn't been looking for guidance since I'd revealed my identity to her, even if it had been an accident. Best damn accident to ever happen.

We fell into a schedule of working, catching lunch together when we could and spending at least every other night together. I was working on finding a replacement for the online counseling so we could spend every night together, but just like the search for a new receptionist, it was coming up with horrible candidates. As much as I wanted to be rid of Mariah and the strain she put on Alix and my relationship, she was a good secretary and I refused to hire someone else who was less qualified simply to ease Alix's mind. There was nothing between Mariah and me anymore and there never would be. Alix had to learn to trust me outside of the bedroom as much as she trusted me in it. Plus, if I hired someone below par, I'd have to spend a lot more time training them and getting them caught up with how I liked things done. It certainly would cut into the time I had free to spend with Alix and that was the last thing I wanted to do.

As the months passed, I was slowly moving a few of my things into Alix's place and she into mine so it was easier for both of us to simply head to work after spending the night together. I had decided it was time to take Alix back to the club. We'd been spending our time in exploring all the ins and outs of each other we'd missed out on in the beginning of our relationship, but I felt it was time to get back to her fear of others.

I brought it up one morning when we were both getting ready for work at my place. We'd had sex in the shower only moments before so her skin was still flushed; her eyes gleamed bright in the mirror.

"Precious?" I asked leaning my towel-covered hips against the counter. She was standing nude in front of me, slathering her beautiful body with lotion before putting on her garter belt.

"Yes?" She looked at me briefly before sitting on the tub ledge and slowly rolling a stocking up one leg.

"Tonight we're going out after work, so make sure you don't get too worn out today." My cock expanded as she moved to pull on the other stocking. It didn't matter that I watched her dress every morning. There was something sexy about the way she clothed herself so carefully, especially when I knew I would be the one taking everything back off her later.

Once she had both stockings on, she stood and attached to them to the garter belt in seconds. She reached for her panties next and I grabbed them from her.

"Not today. You will go without." The flash in her eyes had my cock so hard it was like I hadn't spilled in her only minutes before.

"Yes, sir," she breathed. "I can't wait for tonight."

"Good. Now get on your knees." I dropped the towel and wrapped a hand around my cock, sliding it up and down while watching as she complied. "Make me come so I'm not hard all day thinking about what I'm going to do to you."

She instantly sucked me into her mouth and moaned around my hot, hard flesh as it slid all the way to the back of her throat. In the months we'd been together she'd learned exactly what I liked and used it to her advantage. Her fingers caressed my balls and her teeth lightly scraped against my shaft as she bobbed her head.

Sinking my hand into her wet locks, I watched her lips stretch over me, leaving me wet as she slid off, her cheeks hollowed as she sucked. I could see her bare breast jiggling with her movements and her stocking-clad thighs spread wide to balance herself. Fucking magnificent.

When a finger slipped behind my balls to press on my taint, teasing my perineum, I groaned. All the muscles in my neck strained as I fought to hold onto my control; no matter how good it felt, I refused to lose it until the very last second. Control is what made me the man I was and I refused to relinquish it, even to the woman I was coming to love more with every passing second. It was no longer an idea that floated around in the corners of my mind, but one that was in thick, bold font and constantly right in front. I loved Alix. I couldn't say the words to her, not when she was awake, but I showed her with every gesture I could.

With the sight of her on her knees and those three little words in my head, my release shot down her throat and she greedily sucked it out of me, making sure she got every drop of it. She even licked her lips once she pulled off me. She stared up at me, a smile lifting the corners of her mouth before she lowered her ass to her heels, waiting for me to tell her what to do next.

I hooked a finger under her chin and brought her gaze to mine again.

"I wish I could take you back to the room and show you how damn good that felt, but we don't have time unless both of us want to be late. Since I don't want either of us not to get off work on time, I don't think that'd be a good idea." I watched a frown mar her beautiful face as I held a hand down to help her to her feet. Pulling her against me as soon as she was up, I wrapped my arms around her waist. "I'll make it up to you tonight. Plus, you know how much hotter it is when I make you wait for it."

"I do, Master." Her voice was raspy as she breathed the words.

"Get dressed then, Precious." I walked out of the room to dress in the closet where all my suits hung. She joined me moments later, having put on her bra. We dressed together, sneaking glances at each other the whole time. Once we were ready, we rode the elevator down to the lobby where I kissed her until she was moaning and writhing against me. Then I went to my office. I'd had Mariah adjust my scheduling to match Alix's so we had more time together in the mornings.

"Morning." Mariah smiled as she stood from her spot behind the desk when I entered.

"Morning." I was surrounded by her perfume as I drew closer. "Any messages?"

"Not so far, sir. Would you like a coffee?" she asked, peering up through her lashes at me.

"Sure. Show my first client in when they get here." I went to prepare for my day. Mariah brought me my mug filled with coffee exactly as I preferred it. Leaning a hip against the corner of my desk as she was known to do, she ran a hand over my shoulder.

"You have a busy day ahead of you. A lot of people needing your assistance lately." She tossed her hair, bringing a new wave of her scent to me. "Let me know if there's anything I can do to make it easier for you."

She often touched me in one way or another and while at first it annoyed me, I simply ignored it since it was always a casual touch.

"Okay." I dismissed her as I lifted my mug to take a sip while reading over notes from my previous session with my first patient. She waited a beat as if expecting more of a response, but when she didn't get it, she left.

At lunch time, she offered to bring me back food since I'd had one patient run over on their time and was behind. I agreed and ate when I had free moments. By the time the end of the day rolled around, I was more than ready for my evening with Alix. The release would be good to help ease the stress of the day.

When I was putting everything up for the night, Mariah came in to let me know she was leaving and I nodded, barely acknowledging her.

"Sir?" she asked, making me stop and look at her.

"Yes?" I didn't know why she insisted on calling me sir, but it was another issue I'd grown tired of addressing. She was stubborn, and really it wasn't all that uncommon of a term outside of the BDSM community.

"It's just…" She trailed off and ducked her head.

"What is it?" I grew aggravated with the delay.

"It's just your… hair." She smiled shyly.

I frowned and ran my hands through my hair to fix whatever was wrong with it.

"Here let me." She held up a hand cautiously and I sighed and gave a slight nod. Whatever would make her let me finish up faster.

She stepped behind me and I tilted my head back so she could reach my hair more easily, since she was shorter than me even with her huge heels on. Her hand glided through my hair once, twice, and I felt a slight brush on my neck. I stepped away from her.

"That's fine. I'll fix it later." I returned to my paperwork. I looked up as she walked toward the door.

"See you tomorrow, sir."

I shook my head at her as I wrapped up for the day. Only moments later, I locked up and headed to meet Alix. She was waiting with a smile on her face when I entered the lobby. I couldn't help but return the look of joy.

"Precious," I said, and immediately took her into my arms. It was like taking the first deep breath I'd been able to get since I'd left her in the morning. "I missed you."

"Mmm, me too," she sighed, holding me as tightly as I held her.

"Let's go before I take you upstairs, or we'll never make it out tonight." It was generally what happened. We'd go straight upstairs, barely making it in the door before we were naked enough to fuck against the wall or floor or any other surface that happened to be near. The few times we went to her house it was only after we'd gone to my apartment for a round or two and to pick up a change of clothes for me since I'd be spending the night at her place. We couldn't keep our hands off each other, even when we weren't having sex. If I had to work, she would have her feet in my lap while watching a movie. Our feet played when we ate and talked. I had to feel her against me in one way or another when we were together.

Threading my fingers with hers, we headed to my car. We each talked about our day as we drove to the club. I hadn't told her where we were headed, but seemed to know from the way she squirmed in her seat more and more the closer we got.

"Mmm, it's been a while. I was wondering if you were ever going to bring me back here." She nodded toward the club when I pulled in the parking lot.

"Did you want to come back?" I held my breath waiting for her answer. If she said no, we'd leave, but I really wanted to take her inside, have her out of her element again.

"Yes, Master. I have been dreaming about it." Her voice was soft, yet easy to hear in the confines of the car.

"Then let's go see what I have planned for you." I jumped from the car and opened her door for her. Placing my hand on the small of her back, we walked side by side into the club. She willingly handed over her purse before we went to my room. I stopped her in the small dressing room. "Prepare yourself for me here. You have two minutes to be on the square."

She nodded and was stripping out of her work clothes before I closed the door to the rest of the room. I went to the other side of the room and removed my coat. Not thirty seconds later she was entered with her head bowed. She moved in her heels to the padded square and knelt down. In just her garter belt, thigh highs and heels she looked fantastic and my cock answered by filling with blood and throbbing. Her hair was down, hanging loose, sensually dancing along her skin.

I grabbed the collar I'd only used on her once before and moved to stand in front of her. She still wore my pearls, but I craved a thicker, more obvious sign she was taken. Stepping behind her, I dragged my finger from shoulder to shoulder, pulling her hair along to drape it over one. I secured the thick black collar around her neck tightly enough that it almost cut off her breathing, but not quite. That pleasure was all mine when I chose to use it.

"Take off my shoes," I instructed her as I moved back in front of her. I preferred to scene barefoot. She

RACHAEL ORMAN

carefully removed one, then the other, before dropping her hands back to her thighs. "Socks too."

Once she'd taken them off, I helped her to her feet and looked right into her beautiful eyes. I couldn't stand to look at the top of subs' heads and didn't know why other Doms would want to.

"Remove my cufflinks." I held up each hand in turn for her to remove them. Setting them on the nearby dresser, I rolled my sleeves up my forearms, then hooked a metal chain to the front of Alix's collar. "Come."

I led her to the main play room, which was filled with people.

There were many seating areas, but I wasn't much for conversation when I had my sexy sub with me. Instead, I led her to a large wooden cross. A couple was currently using it, so I sat and pulled Alix into my lap. The last time we'd watched people use the cross Alix had gotten so excited, I didn't mind waiting our turn.

"A little show before it's your turn up there," I told her, rubbing a palm up and down her leg, teasing the skin at the top of her thigh highs. "Watch them. See if you can figure out what I have in mind for you."

It was part of what I missed about the club. The ability to watch and be watched. Alix loved it almost as much as I did. By the time the couple exited the stage, she was wiggling on my lap, rubbing against my erection. Unluckily for her, I'd taken a few moments in the bathroom at work to jerk off just before I started getting ready to leave so I wasn't so on edge when we played.

While my control was strong, I also knew my limitations, and Alix was good at pushing them when she let me completely dominate her.

Taking hold of the leash, I led her to the cross with her facing it.

"Hands up." I restrained her wrists with the leather straps attached to the top before pushing her feet farther apart with my own. Her ankles were secured with the ones on the bottom, keeping her in a perfect X to torment. I stepped back and smiled while drinking her in. Perfection — well, almost. I only needed to bring some color to her pale skin and it really would be. I grabbed a flogger that was nearby for just such a use. It was thin-strapped and would sting more than the thicker ones.

We didn't have a safeword. I didn't work that way. No was no and would always be in my world.

I stepped close to her, feeling the heat of her penetrate my shirt. Normally I took it off, but the feel of her skin on mine was always distracting. I wanted nothing deterring my plans, even myself.

When I planted a soft kiss on her neck, she moaned and canted her head slightly to offer more skin to me. I rubbed my erection against her before moving back again. Softly, I trailed the end of the leather over her skin and smirked when she shivered, goosebumps popping out over every inch of her flesh.

After trailing the ends of the flogger over her a few times, I brought it down with a sharp flick of my wrist. Instantly a lovely blush bloomed over her back and she groaned. Spreading my feet, I picked up a comfortable eight pattern as I covered her upper back, arms and buttocks. Her cries of pain turned to moans of pleasure as she found subspace. I stopped when my shoulder started to ache. The flogger had turned her skin a bright red and would likely even leave a few bruises. The sight had my cock hard and pulsing against my zipper while leaving a damp spot where its eagerness seeped out.

I released the straps from her ankles first; she moved them unsteadily under her as I moved to undo the ones around her wrists. Once she was free, I scooped her into my arms. Her head rested against my chest right where I wanted it; I carried her back to my room and settled her on the bed. Removing my shirt, I climbed in next to her and gently caressed her back while rubbing on some ointment that would help reduce the soreness the next day.

Eventually, she came around and looked up to smile at me. I brushed stray hair off her face and kissed her lips softly.

"Welcome back, Precious."

"Mmm, I love when you make me soar," she murmured in a sleepy voice. It always took a while to fully come back to yourself so I kept touching her, easing her way.

"I love to make you fly, baby. Hell, I just love when you hand your control over to me. It's absolutely the most exciting thing you could ever do to me."

"Well, I don't have to try to excite you in other ways then." She smiled as she said it and I laughed softly at her.

"You excite me with everything you do, but that doesn't mean you should stop trying to find something new you want to try out on me." There was plenty we hadn't done when it came to BDSM, but when it came to anything vanilla I was pretty sure we had that covered. I welcomed her presenting something she wanted to try, as she had yet to request something or say she specifically wanted a particular act. While I liked to be in control, I wanted her to know nothing was off-limits for me. I would do anything to keep her happy and in my arms.

Lost in my own thoughts, I was jolted when she yanked herself away from me. I looked at her, surprised and a bit shocked at the sudden move. She sat up in the bed and pulled the sheet over her body, which she had never done before in my presence.

"What's wrong?" I asked, looking around the room to see what had caused the sudden change.

"You have lipstick on your neck." Every muscle in her body grew taut as her eyes locked on my neck and her eyes turned ice cold.

"What?"

"Lipstick. On your neck. Who has been kissing your neck? I know it wasn't me. I didn't have lipstick on today and I haven't kissed your neck. I didn't notice it before when you picked me up so it must have been under your collar." She moved off the bed, yanking the sheet with her as she moved away from me. Accusation was clear in her stance, but I was truly lost. I didn't know how it got there and I didn't think she'd take that for an excuse.

"I have no idea. Really. Baby, come back to bed so we can talk about this," I pleaded, holding a hand out to her.

"No. I want to leave, right now." She dropped the sheet and disappeared into the dressing room. By the time I'd pulled on my shirt and folded my jacket over my arm, she still hadn't returned, so I knocked once on the door before pushing it open. The dressing room was empty. She'd left.

Growling in frustration, I ran down the hall to see her slip out the front door with her purse over her shoulder. I slammed the front door and the door-man glared at me, but I ignored him as I looked for where Alix had gone. Just as I spotted her, she vanished into the backseat of one of the cabs outside the club. I tried to get to the cab before it took off, but wasn't fast enough.

She was gone.

<u>Chapter 13</u>

Alix

I was running. I knew it, but I couldn't stop myself. There was no way I could face him as my mind whirled out of control. After such a deep experience, only to find another woman's lipstick on his neck — my world shattered. There is only one way lipstick gets beneath the collar of a dress shirt. I couldn't hear his excuses. I couldn't let him make me believe again.

The last few months I'd put up with numerous other signs that other women would add up to something suspicious, but after his vehemence about not cheating the first time, I had let it all go, against my better judgement.

However, I couldn't let go of the lipstick. I couldn't. As soon as I got home, I locked the door and actually hid in my closet. I didn't want to go near my bed, or couch, or anywhere else in the house John and I had been together. I needed to be alone.

All my life I'd been made to feel like I'd never be enough, but that had changed with John. I had this beautiful period of time where I felt like I could be what he needed, what he wanted — that I was enough. The world crumpled down around me with thoughts of all the times he'd come to me smelling of other women, the stories I heard from his ex, the way she so brazenly showed too much cleavage or thigh in the office. She touched him and he let her, even in front of me. He hadn't been trying so hard to hide what was going on, but I'd been the naïve one that let him pull the cloth over my eyes in more ways than one.

I'd been so desperate to believe him that I didn't trust myself and what I was seeing with my own eyes.

My strength and confidence, which had built over the time we'd been together, was leached away by the thoughts of deceit and lies. I hid in the closet trying to keep the outside world at bay for as long as I could, even long after my legs and butt begged me to move. My needy bladder was what finally broke me.

After relieving myself, I went about my house straightening things, trying to find some sense of normalcy where nothing else was okay. When I plugged my phone into the charger, I saw I had a slew of missed calls and texts. I didn't bother checking them. They would be from John and I didn't have the heart to face him.

In fact, I didn't find the strength to face him for over two weeks. I called in sick, stating a family emergency, even though I had no family worth missing a single day of work for. Since I never took a vacation, I had more than enough paid time to use. The entire two weeks I stayed holed up in my apartment. I was barely eating, so I didn't need to go to the store to get food.

At the end of two weeks, I felt no better than I had when I started the time away, so it was with a heavy heart that I started looking for new employment. I loved where I worked, but I refused to stay where I would be forced to see the man who'd broken my heart.

When I returned to work, I put on heavy makeup to help cover the bags under my eyes and the fact I'd lost some weight. The only person who noticed was Jennifer, and even though she peppered me with questions, I shrugged them off with single-word answers or ignored them altogether. Finally she got the hint that I didn't want to talk and left me alone.

After having so much time off, I was booked solid, one appointment straight into another. The following week I'd be running to keep up with all the events that were booked, but it was good. The more work I had to do, the less time my brain could dedicate to rehashing the same thoughts that had been circling in my head.

I was broken.

My old, comforting habits came back. I found myself escaping more than four times a day to the bathroom while at work to masturbate. I couldn't do it in my office as my appointments were too closely booked. There was no pleasure from it, but I found it helped bring a tiny bit of my old self back. Memories of doing the same thing for many years brought me comfort that I was still me. I was still okay in some small corner of my brain.

I didn't think about John during those times; I knew he'd be mad at me if he knew, but I was mad at him so all it ended up doing was making me twist and pinch myself painfully, making it harder to get off on the next trip I made to the bathroom.

I made it over a week back at work before I spotted him. Since he'd tailored his hours to mine when we were together I knew when he'd be coming or going and made sure to be out of sight at those times. I had appointments well into the night as I tried to play catch-up, and one night when I was cleaning up to leave, it was after ten when I looked up and spotted him.

He hadn't seen me and I ducked behind my desk. As usual, he was dressed impeccably in a suit and an all-knowing smile that made every woman drool over him. Every woman but me. It tore my heart out to see he looked as good as he had the day I'd left.

Once I was sure he was gone, I collapsed into my chair and fought to hold back the tears that threatened for the first time in weeks. I hadn't cried for him. I refused to. Too many times I had let tears fall for myself. Obviously even after months of my full dedication to him, I wasn't enough, and that's all I had to offer him. Tears would do nothing to change it.

Grabbing my purse, I locked my office and walked through the lobby. Jennifer waved me over.

"Alix, you need a night out. Let's go get wasted and relax some. Come on, it'll be a good time. You *need* a good time," she pleaded with me. She'd been begging me to tell her what was going on. She'd deduced that whatever had been between John and I had ended, but hadn't pushed for details. She really was becoming a friend and showing me she wanted to be there for me.

"I don't know," I sighed. I was exhausted, but I was constantly that way since I couldn't sleep.

"It'll help you feel human again, I promise. We'll leave when you want to leave. Just get out of your house and office for a few hours." She clasped her hands together and pushed out her bottom lip in a pout.

"Okay, as long as we leave when I say I want to leave." I gave in as a loud, annoying burst of feminine laughter filled the lobby. The sound was familiar and made my blood freeze. Turning on my heel, I spotted Mariah. She was dazzling as usual. Her hair sparkled in the lights as she moved, her makeup looking spotless as her tight dress hugged every curve of her perfect body that was elongated by spiked heels. She held a phone to her ear as she moved through the open room.

"I can't wait, sir. I'm on my way up to you. I don't need dinner, I need you after the long day we had." She paused as if listening to something on the other end of the line. "Absolutely, sir. I want to be so sore I can't sit down tomorrow without remembering having you over me. It'll keep my panties wet and praying you'll ask me to come into your office for a session of our own."

I closed my eyes as she moved far enough away I couldn't hear her as she waited for the elevator.

"Yeah, I think I need a drink," I told Jennifer, who gave me a sad smile as she collected her things.

We went to her house, where I refused to change into one of her ridiculous outfits. Instead, I shed my jacket, figuring the tank top I had on underneath would work fine. It was a bit see-through, but I wore a bra so there wasn't much to show. After trading out my skirt for a pair of her jeans, I deemed myself ready. My hair was pulled up into a tight bun since I refused to wear it down. Anything that would normally please John, I did the opposite. I didn't want to attract him; I didn't even want to think about him.

Jennifer pulled on a skimpy skirt that showed off her body before fluffing her hair. She took me to a bar that wasn't far. I'd never been there, but I hadn't been in ninety percent of the local bars. Once we made it through the crowd, we both sat on stools along the bar top.

As usual, Jennifer held the conversation through our first two drinks. The woman could talk, and talk she did. I was thankful she wasn't relying upon me to really answer or interact to keep up the flow of chatter since my head was a mess. After our first two drinks, though, I felt everything loosening and relaxing for the first time in weeks. Halfway through our third drink, I found myself talking about John.

"I miss him," I slurred slightly before taking another pull off my drink.

"Go get your man then." Jennifer acted as if it was so simple.

"I can't. I'm pretty sure he's fucking his secretary and I'm nothing compared to her." I leaned my elbows on the table as I shook my head.

"I don't even need to see her to know you're better than her." Jennifer looked me up and down even though she couldn't see my lower half, which was hidden by the table. "You just don't see how amazing you are."

"Wait until you see her. You'll see what I'm talking about. Plus, I don't need a man who cheats. Even if she *is* better looking than me, he should have the balls to break up with me first." I glared at my drink, seeing his face in it. I slammed back what was left in the glass so I didn't have to see it anymore.

"You're right there, girl. No woman should have to put up with a cheater." She waved her arm for another round.

We had moved away from the bar to a small table so our conversation wouldn't be heard by everyone.

"Since you're over, you have to tell me… Is he packing heat? Or is it all for show?" Her glossy eyes dilated. I could tell she was thinking about all the naughty things she wanted to do to him between the sheets. Jealousy flared inside me, but I shoved it back since I no longer had any rights to him.

"Yeah, he's got it all and then some," I sighed, feeling the need to give her some juicy details even though it tugged at my heart to talk about how amazing he fucked. He was likely bending his little secretary over and doing all the things he used to do to me to her. "He's good in every way."

"Aw, it was supposed to be a joke, not make you feel worse. Sorry, I'm not good at break-up chat." Jennifer's grin was replaced by a frown, making her look awkward. Frowning wasn't something she did often, while I'd mastered the face. "Let's drink until you forget who he even is."

And we did. Almost. I don't think I could physically drink enough to forget the man who owned my heart, not and still be breathing anyway. Somehow I made it back to my place. The last part of the night was scattered bits and pieces as the alcohol took over, robbing me of the memories.

I had to work the next day so going out and getting so completely blitzed probably wasn't the best idea. Sitting on my couch nursing a water to hopefully ward off a hangover in the morning, I stared at my computer. I really needed someone to talk to. I had no one I could really tell everything to. Jennifer would likely understand, but then she'd admitted to not being good with men and the complications that came with them since she didn't hang around long enough for them to arise.

Finally I blew out a long breath and pulled up the online counseling site. It had been a long time since I'd used it, since I'd felt like I had a good handle on life, but everything was crashing down and it was the one place I could go to not be judged while being completely open.

Counselor21: Good evening. Or should I say morning? How have you been?

BadKitty2: Not so well.

Counselor21: What changed? You were gone for a while, so I assume everything was good then.

BadKitty2: He cheated.

Counselor21: Did you talk to him about it or catch him in the act?

BadKitty2: No.

Counselor21: Then how do you know?

BadKitty2: Call it a woman's intuition.

Counselor21: That's it? Just a hunch?

BadKitty2: Hunches can be more telling than the heart or brain, which are easily swayed.

Counselor21: But do you have anything to support your hunch?

BadKitty2: I do. Lipstick on his neck. Wasn't mine.

Counselor21: Anything else?

BadKitty2: Rumors. Overheard people talking.

Counselor21: I really think what you need to do is sit down and talk to him about it. Let him know why you are feeling the way you are. See if he can give any explanations or put your worries to rest. I'm not saying he is or isn't, but at least give him the chance to have his say. If after your conversation you still feel he is cheating maybe it would be best to take a break.

BadKitty2: You're crazier than I am! Like he'd just admit it.

Counselor21: Not necessarily, but it gives you the chance to look into his face as he lies (or tells the truth) and *that* is where you'll get your answer.

BadKitty2: Yeah, maybe. Thanks.

Counselor21: It's what I'm here for.

I logged off the computer feeling better than I had in days. The counselor was right. I could look at John and tell if he was hiding something as I told him what I knew. I would go see him during lunch when he'd be stuck in the office and unable to turn things against me and my possibly treacherous body. It wouldn't be easy to face him, but it might help the ache that lived in my chest, or help get me some closure.

I fell into bed and prayed the next time I was there I'd have more peace of mind while being on the path to getting over the biggest heartbreak of my life. Did I think he could possibly be telling the truth about not cheating? In some small corner of my mind, I did. However, it was easier to focus on the worst outcome because it was what I expected in life.

In the morning, I dressed carefully for work, taking extra time on my hair and makeup, wanting to look as well put-together as I could for such a heavy conversation. My

155

hands shook, my knees were weak and I had bags under my eyes from not sleeping well since I'd left him, but after a few layers of concealer at least one problem was less noticeable.

The early hours of work ticked by and I chewed at my nails as I stared at the clock. Finally lunch rolled around and I grabbed my purse before hustling through the lobby. I wanted to get it over with. The door to his office slammed open unintentionally and I looked at Mariah behind her desk. She sent me a bright smile of triumph.

"Oh, Alix. I don't believe John was expecting you. He's super busy and plain exhausted. I've worn him out today." She sighed contentedly and ran her fingers through her hair, which was oddly out of place and tangled. She smirked as she hastily brought it back to order and the door to John's office opened.

Glancing up, I sucked in a breath. John stood, shocked, with one hand on the door, the other resting on the frame.

"Alix," he whispered.

"John." I crossed my arms over my chest when he reached a hand toward me. His hand fell short and he turned abruptly to Mariah.

"I need my messages and a new notepad — for some reason the one I have is mangled," he told her before turning back to me. "Let me reschedule this patient, then I'll be free."

"I'll wait." I turned jerkily on my heel and sat in one of the vacant chairs.

Mariah jumped up and rushed to get the items he requested before handing them over. They spoke in hushed tones for a moment before he returned to the office and she glared at me.

"Well, I guess I'm taking an early lunch." Mariah scowled as she retrieved her purse from under the desk. She stepped around the desk to stop in front of me. "If he's looking for his briefcase, it's under my desk."

I nodded, looking not at her but at the door John was behind. She left the office and minutes later a couple exited his office, leaving the door slightly ajar.

"Alix?" I heard him call out. "I have to find my briefcase and then I'm taking the afternoon off to spend with you."

"You don't have to do that. I just need a few minutes." I stood and moved behind the desk to grab his briefcase.

"We have a lot to talk about. I don't want to be worried about appointments. They can be moved." His voice carried out from his office as I heard rustling.

As I wrapped my hand around the handle of the briefcase, my eyes locked on something in the trash can right next to it. A condom. A *used* condom. *What the fuck?* I back pedaled as my heart thumped in my chest. It couldn't be. I didn't need any other conversation, that one item told me enough. John said he didn't have sex in his office, and I knew he didn't allow his patients to either, so there was only one way that condom came to be there. He really was fucking Mariah. It was the only conclusion I could come up with as my vision greyed and pain swarmed over me. Dropping the case, I ran for the door.

"Damn it. Not again!" I heard John yell from behind me, but I didn't stop until I was in a cab parked in front of the hotel.

My heart was breaking and I couldn't handle seeing him attempt to deny everything straight to my face. I didn't think the pain could get any worse than it had been, but I was wrong. So wrong.

When it had been a possibility, I had held on to a shred of hope things could be fixed, but not after knowing he was fucking her where he'd refused to fuck me. I couldn't handle it. There was absolutely nothing left to salvage. Nothing left to repair. It was gone in a matter of seconds. A chance glimpse of something I was never supposed to see.

Chapter 14

John

This was it. Alix was in my office. It'd been painfully hard for me to play an impartial party when she'd shown up for online counseling the night before. I had followed her to the bar and made sure she returned home by herself. If she had tried to bring someone home with her I probably would've gone insane, but she didn't. She was alone when she arrived at her place and I sat in my car just feet from her to act as her counselor, the exact reason I had a mobile hotspot. I had no idea where she'd gotten the idea I was cheating on her, except for the lipstick, which confused me still. Unfortunately, she wasn't willing to divulge such information online.

As hard as it was, I tried to go about my normal business meeting with clients the following day, but when she'd shown up I'd told the couple in my office I had a family emergency that needed to be handled immediately and they'd understood. I'd dismissed Mariah so it'd only be the two of us. I was to the point where I was willing to do something I'd never once in my life done — get down on my knees and beg her to let me try to explain.

Then before I could even get everything gathered and secured so I could spend the rest of the day with her, she was gone. Just that fast something had spooked her and she'd run from me again.

I couldn't help but notice in the brief moments when I'd laid eyes on her, that she'd still been wearing my pearls; somewhere deep within her, she still belonged to me. It was the only thing that gave me the strength to turn from her. I wished I hadn't.

While I didn't know exactly what it was that had spooked her, it broke the last, lonely piece of me free of the control I normally held so dear. I could feel the last essences of myself spiral out of reach into the dark, warped zone I'd been living in since she'd discovered the lipstick on my neck. The lipstick smudge I still couldn't figure out.

The last vestige of me disappeared and I felt the deep, dark past surge over me, taking me to a place I hadn't visited in a long time. A horrible state of mind I'd hoped never to revisit, but the loss of the single thing that matter to me, broke me. My carefully constructed world of control collapsed under the strain of my splintered heart.

I was no longer the man I strove and struggled to be, but the broken, abused child I'd grown up as. My knees gave way as I collapsed to the floor, gasping for breath. Feelings I'd banished surged forward to engulf me.

Before I knew what I was doing, I was driving at a high rate of speed. Swerving my car through the other meaningless beings going about their boring lives, I had only one place I needed to be. The only place that would help me find some peace of mind. I didn't want to go there, but I couldn't stop myself.

My mind screamed for me for me to turn around and chase Alix, but the meager pieces I could pull together knew I had nothing to offer her. She didn't want the chaos that I was. She deserved a man who was better put together, one who could give himself freely. Someone I'd never be. My youth had been too horrible to leave me whole. I'd given her every part of me that I could, every part of me that deserved to be shared with the world, but it had gone horribly wrong somewhere.

I couldn't think of the dominant I'd become to control the world. Couldn't think of the multi-degreed professional. No, seeing the love of my life run from me like I was the scum of the earth made me feel like I was back to the child who deserved every punishment he received because he couldn't do good enough.

Pulling into the parking lot of Scene, I shrugged out of my coat and removed my cufflinks before exiting my car. I wasn't there to play Dom. I was there for something I hadn't sought in years.

Punishment.

Alix's rejection was a punishment in one form but I was looking for another type that I couldn't get anywhere else.

When I walked in, I handed over my wallet and keys and requested a Dom. The woman behind the counter flushed, but nodded, handing me a pair of leather cuffs to put around my wrists to let everyone know that I was a submissive seeking a dominant.

Once I entered the playroom, it didn't take long for me to start getting offers. Before I could accept any of them, though, I was interrupted by my friend, the owner of Scene, Gabe.

"What the hell do you think you're doing?" he barked at me, crossing his arms over his wide chest.

"I don't know what you mean, sir." I dropped to my knees and bowed my head.

His fingers slipped into my short hair, but somehow managed to grip it tightly enough to jerk my head back so I looked at him.

"You are a Dom, not a sub. What kind of game are you playing here?" Gabe growled fiercely at me, lowering his face toward mine.

"No, sir. I am here as a submissive looking for a dominant tonight," I breathed, arching into the burn sparking in my scalp as he pulled harder. I didn't expect him to remember my past, as I was hesitant to share it with anyone. However, I had told him years ago every detail of my past while he whipped me; even then he didn't believe I had the capability to be a submissive, but I'd shown him I did that night.

"What the fuck, John? Snap out of this shit. You haven't needed the whip in years, why now? Talk to me," he pleaded, releasing my hair to rub both hands over his face.

"NO," I yelled loudly, drawing the attention of those around me. "I don't wish to speak of it. I need to forget, sir."

Gabe let out a heavy sigh and nodded. He knew he wasn't going to talk me out of it.

"I'll let Munch know." Gabe strode out of the room. Munch wasn't the man's real name, it was his Dom name. He was a sadist and he very much so enjoyed doling out as much pain as a submissive could take.

"Well, well. Look at the little bitch who needs a few licks of my whip." I knew it was Munch from the previous encounters we'd had. "Get to my cross now, you worthless piece of shit."

Finally I felt peace settle over my mind as I fully handed over my control to him. I didn't have to think, I simply had to act, to do as instructed. Munch knew my submissive needed the humiliation to feel complete. I couldn't completely submit until I was made to feel as low as possible.

Scrambling to my feet, I moved toward the cross until I felt a heavy boot kick out my knee, making me fall to all fours.

"Did I say you could walk? Do you think you are worthy of being at my height? No, you aren't, you lazy son of a bitch." Munch followed as I crawled to the stage that was specifically his.

I could feel eyes on me, people watching me. I closed my eyes, letting the shame sink in.

Once I reached the stage, I clambered onto it and waited to be told I could stand. Munch grabbed an ear and yanked me to my feet while a groan slipped from my lips.

"On the cross now, boy." Munch released me and pain radiated through the side of my face from where he'd tugged. I positioned myself with arms and legs spread wide so he could shackle me to the heavy, wooden cross.

Stepping back, he held a knife in my face, dragging it along my cheek.

"Don't move or I'll be forced to show you how sharp this is." He moved the knife to the collar of my shirt and made quick work of slicing through it, then each of my sleeves. It fell to the ground in a heap of scraps. Using the sharp point, he trailed it over my skin to randomly push it into me, but not enough to draw blood. "Think that since you are grown now you're some bad shit, don't you?"

"No, sir," I murmured and gasped when he pushed harder against me.

"Worked out to get all this muscle. Did you think that would make you stronger than me?" Munch moved the knife to my neck.

"No, sir. Never, sir." I shivered against the cold metal that could easily end my life at that moment.

"That's right. You'll always be my little bitch. I'll always own you." Munch knew my history, knew exactly the buttons to push that would drag my mind to the darkest of places. It was why I needed to be punished, to submit, to have my control taken away. There was only one way I knew how to handle extreme emotions, and that was to have them tamed for me by the slash of a whip and the fear of a knife.

Removing the knife from my neck, I felt the absence of his heat as he stepped away. A loud thud on the floor made my muscles tense. I knew what was coming and it was impossible to relax.

There was a slight whir and swish as the air moved before the loud crack as leather met skin. The tip of the whip slapped harshly against my back and I arched from the pain that shot through me.

"Mmm, it's been awhile since this lily-white skin has been touched by the kiss of a whip." Munch laughed a deep, nasty laugh. "That all changes now."

Another lashing, and I cried out from it. My back was on fire, my knees wanted to give out, but there would be no escaping. I was trussed up to the cross, forced to deal with my demons as they raged in my mind. My father, my mother… Alix. Old demons warred with new ones and were more painful than the whip would ever be.

My mind was shattered, a mess of emotions and thoughts.

I lost count of how many times the whip licked across my skin, but eventually my mind calmed, everything fled, replaced by pain. The world slowed and clouded to a place where nothing mattered.

Munch was pressing against my back, against the welts and bruises he'd caused.

"Come on, boy, time to get off the cross." He released the bindings and wrapped an arm around my shoulders as I stumbled off the stage.

Sitting on a couch, he pulled me next to him.

"Over my lap so I can put salve on you, boy." Munch pulled on my shoulder until I lay over his lap. I could feel his erection press against my hip and whimpered. He brought his palm down on my ass. "Stop moving and making noises or I'll take your ass right here, boy."

"Sorry, sir." He'd fucked me in the past in a scene so I didn't put it past him.

He smoothed thick salve over my back and I couldn't help but squirm as the pain surged.

"Hm, lucky it's your first night back. You're not so good at following instructions, it seems. Next time I won't be so generous." Once he was done, he gently ran a hand over my ass, the other over my hair. It was his version of after care. He could look his fill at the marks he left while giving his sub the comfort they needed. After a long while, he gave one final pat to my ass telling me it was time to get up. "You are dismissed, boy."

I went home feeling much more content than when I'd shown up. So, it became a new part of my daily ritual. I'd check in on Alix as much as I could, but it was tearing my heart open every time I saw her so I needed a way to release the pain, and Munch was perfect at doing it.

For the next week, I'd leave work and visit Munch before visiting Alix as she puttered around her home. She looked as terrible as I felt, but she never answered my calls or texts. Sometimes I would send a text while I watched her just to see her face as she read them. I didn't understand why she wouldn't open up to me, why she couldn't share what was going through her head, and why for the love of God she refused to even tell me what had happened to make her run.

I knew she thought I was cheating, but what was leading her to that conclusion, I couldn't figure out. There wasn't a chance I would touch another woman, not when I'd rather have her in my arms, my bed, my soul. Losing her made every horrible thing I'd lived through seem like child's play. My life hadn't been easy and I didn't think anything could ever hurt me like that again. Alix had gone and proved me wrong. She'd proved there was still so much agony to be felt in the world.

I wanted it to end. All of it. I wanted to go back to the months of complete bliss we'd shared. I'd give anything to return to those times.

Chapter 15

Alix

Another week had passed and I'd survived. John messaged and called me at least every couple of hours, even through the night. At least neither of us was sleeping well. It made me feel a bit better that I wasn't alone in my misery.

After an exhausting day, I found myself parked at Scene. I hadn't meant to go there, but since I had, I unbuckled my seatbelt and headed inside. Maybe submitting to someone else would help me finally start to get over John, since time obviously wasn't doing it. After handing over my purse, I told the woman at the counter that I was an unclaimed submissive and she handed me a pair of leather cuffs to put on to designate me as such.

Walking into the open room, I struggled to keep my breathing calm. I had never been an unclaimed sub or played with anyone else and the idea scared me. However, I refused to back down and let it stop me from giving my all to move on from John and the control he had over me. Just that morning I had finally built myself up to taking off his pearls. The final sign that he was important to me. I felt naked without them, but it was time. Three weeks of self-pity and wallowing was more than enough.

"Looking for someone to play with?" a voice asked from behind me and I spun to find the man I'd seen John nod to many times in passing. He had to know that at one time I was claimed by him.

"Yes, sir." I bowed my head out of respect and he stepped closer.

"What are you looking for tonight?"

"I… I'm not sure, sir," I stuttered, not having thought so far ahead.

"A spanking? A flogging? A whipping? More?" He hooked a finger under my chin, forcing me to meet his gaze.

"A spanking?" I answered, but it came out more as a question than a statement.

"That could be arranged. Do you have a safe word?"

"N...no, sir." We'd never required one and I couldn't think of one on the spot.

"How about red to stop, yellow to pause so we can talk about it?"

"Okay, sir."

"Go to the spanking bench and drop your skirt to your ankles. I'll be right there."

I nodded and dropped my head again before swiftly walking to an unoccupied bench on the opposite side of the room. Swallowing the growing lump of nerves in my throat, I slid my skirt down my thighs to pool around my ankles. I hadn't worn a garter belt and thigh highs; instead I had on regular pantyhose that came all the way up to my waist.

Leaning forward onto the bench, I left my ass in the air while my chest pressed against the hard, ungiving wood.

"Hands," the man demanded when he stepped behind me. I lifted my hands to my lower back and felt rough rope being wrapped around them, securing them together. "Safe words?"

"Red and yellow, sir," I answered automatically.

"You will get twenty then you will sit on your knees until I tell you to get up, understand?"

"Yes, sir."

Something much firmer than his hand slapped against my ass and I cried out. The familiar burn spread over both cheeks at the same time. He had to be using a paddle of some kind. John normally used his hand and I had expected the same from the stranger, but it wasn't more than I could handle.

Again and again the paddle came down. I tried to count in my head, but gave up after losing count the second time. Everything became blurry and I felt the haze of subspace take over. It was a blessed peacefulness I needed. I could breathe again; I wasn't in pain from heartbreak. Oddly, however, the pain didn't morph into a sexual pleasure like it did when John was inflicting it; instead it added another layer of comfort around me. Each time the paddle came down, my panty-hose burned against my skin. I wished I had worn my thigh highs or nothing at all, but it was too late. The added sensation only made it more real, more intense.

Finally I was jostled and forced to move off the bench. My knees pressed into carpet, my skirt still around my ankles. A heavy hand forced me to sit back, my sore ass pressing against my heels.

"I will be back for you. Do *not* move until then or I will spank you all over again with something much worse than a paddle. Understand?" The man pushed a finger into my forehead until I looked up at him.

"Yes, sir," I murmured through the haze. My tongue felt thick and hard to move, but I managed to get the two words out.

"Good girl." He turned and walked from my sight.

I couldn't say how long I sat like that. My knees ached, my back ached and my ass burned like never before, but still the man hadn't returned. It was a cry from a familiar voice that made me lift my head to find where it was coming from.

Everything stopped. The room dropped away and all that was left was the couple in front of me.

John was tethered to a cross while a hulk of a man unleashed a long, snakelike whip, making it snap against John's back. His back was already covered with welts in various stages of healing, but there wasn't an inch of unmarred skin left. Not that it stopped the man from repeatedly laying into him. Just the sound of the leather against his skin made me shiver. It had to hurt, but John simply held his head down and took it without a single sound.

I'd never seen John as a submissive and would happily never witness it again. It was a scary sight. He was no longer the strong, controlled man I loved, but one who was obviously beaten down to the point that he wasn't feeling pain.

When the hulk dropped the whip to the floor and closed in on John, I wanted to run to him, to save him, from what was coming next. He'd had enough in my eyes. I didn't know how he came to be there, but it wasn't right. I couldn't understand.

To my surprise, the man reached around and unbuckled John's slacks and let them fall to the ground before roughly shoving his boxers down as well.

"Not enough pain, bitch?" the man growled as he slapped John's cock.

"No, sir," John moaned. "More. I need more, sir."

I gaped at his words. My brain struggled to understand the side of John I was witnessing. I glanced around to see if anyone else was watching their scene, but oddly there was no one else within hearing distance, as if it was too painful to watch or they'd been warned away.

My eyes burned as I returned them to John. Tears wanted to escape, but I kept them back so they didn't blur my vision. I needed to watch. I needed to let it sear into my brain that there was so much more to the man I thought I knew so well.

Hulk moved to a nearby table and grabbed a bottle of lube. He let some of it slide down the crease of John's ass before he shifted his feet. I could only assume he was taking himself out of his pants, since he pressed against John while whispering words in a harsh tone. They were spoken so low I couldn't hear them, but his stance said it all. They weren't pleasant ones.

"You are going to take me in your body, boy. If you so much as move to escape the pain, I will tear you open, do you understand me? Do you want me to make your tender little hole bleed? Then you'll remember me reaming you for days."

"N...no, sir. I don't want to bleed, sir," John whimpered — actually whimpered. His voice sounded like a little boy's, one who was pleading to be saved, and my heart skipped a beat. I had to dig my fingers into my palms to force myself to stay where I was. He had a safe word; he could make it stop if he truly wanted to.

The man rolled his hips before thrusting against John and from the cry of agony that left him, I knew the man was filling his ass. I audibly gasped as tears finally escaped my eyes. The man turned his head and met my gaze as he pounded into John with a hand around his throat. A harsh smile came over his face before he turned back to John.

"Even your ass can't get it right. No matter how many times I fuck you, all you do is whimper like a little bitch. You are so pathetic. No one will love you. No one will ever care if you live or die because you are so fucking worthless. If you weren't trussed up, I'd make you suck the shit from my dick until I came down your disgusting throat."

173

The man's words made my throat work overtime to keep from releasing my stomach contents. I couldn't stand to watch more. I lowered my head in shame. I was only an observer and yet I couldn't handle it. How he managed to take it I didn't know.

It wasn't the fact he was with another man that confused me, but the fact that he was submitting, that he was being degraded without objection. I couldn't wrap my head around how things had changed so rapidly in his world.

I focused on the burning pain in my ass and knew it was nothing compared to the pain John had to feel from the lashes to his back. I tried to tune out the nasty words spewing from the man fucking John. It seemed to last forever before I felt a gentle hand on my shoulder. Glancing up, I found it was the man who'd spanked me.

"Come, little one," he said in a soft tone. I stood and he helped me pull up my skirt before ushering me out of the room. He led me down the hall filled with doorways I knew led to private rooms until he finally pushed one open and followed me in. "Sit."

I eyed the room, which appeared to be an office, as he sat in one of the chairs and waved a hand at the other.

"Alix, I'm Gabe. I'm the owner of Scene. Please sit. I need to talk to you. It is very important."

I eyed him cautiously feeling more nervous than I had out in the playroom.

"If you care at all for John, you will want to hear what I have to say."

My heart thudded harder in my chest when he mentioned John. He had information about him. I needed to know what it was. Pulling the chair a bit farther away, I sat facing him.

"Good. Now I trust you witnessed the scene going on out there, correct?" He crossed an ankle over the opposite knee, relaxing back into his seat.

"Yes."

"John has been here every day for the last week. Sometimes multiple times a day. He's suffering. He is punishing himself in the only way he knows how. It helps calm his demons, but it also gives him a new pain to focus on since he can't control the other pain he's dealing with. I don't know exactly what is going on between the two of you, but I suspect you can help him more than he is allowing me to at this time." Gabe dropped his leg and leaned his elbows on his knees.

"I...I don't know what I can do." I shook my head in denial.

"Talk to him. See if he will share what it is that's eating at him. It's something personal. I might know his past, but something set him off. Something pushed him over the edge and he doesn't even seem to be trying to control it. He's lost in his head, in his demons, his pain." Gabe ran a tired hand over his face. "I've tried. Every time he shows up here, I try to get him to open up, but he refuses. He won't talk about it."

"You think he'd talk to me?" I shifted in my seat, my sore ass rubbing against my skirt.

"I don't know. It can't hurt. While it seems the two of you are no longer Dom and sub, he had a connection to you that I've never seen him have with anyone before. I've known John for quite a few years, too, so I know it's not something to be taken lightly. Please, if you care for him, try. Try, not because I'm asking, but for him." Gabe reached across the space to clasp my hand in his. "Please."

I sighed. I didn't know if John would talk to me. What if it was me that had caused him to go over the edge? I didn't think I could handle the guilt. It might not have been my fault I'd left, but I hadn't allowed him to talk to me about it. Maybe giving him that chance would help. Maybe if I pushed to know what was going on in other areas of his life, he would talk. I would try, because I couldn't stand seeing him hurt so much.

"I'll go see him at his office tomorrow," I told Gabe, who released a sigh as his shoulders relaxed.

"Thank you. I will be indebted to you. John is a good friend and I don't like seeing him this way. As for you little miss, you need to be more careful about which Doms you play with. No matter what happens with John, you need to learn to set clearer boundaries if you're going to scene with new Doms. Talk about limits before you scene. You could've easily been put in a hairy situation real quick. Luckily, I spotted you when you came in and made sure you were here to witness John's scene since it was the only way you'd understand how much pain he's in."

"Understood." I stood with a nod. I couldn't sit in the office anymore. I needed privacy to build the courage to enter John's office in the morning. Needed to plan what I was going to say to him.

Gabe walked with me until I turned to leave and he returned to the main room. The urge to look and see if John was still on the stage nearly had me following him, but I forced myself to leave instead.

After another restless night, I found myself dressed in a pantsuit, hair in a severe low ponytail, and heading into John's office shortly after he'd passed through the lobby.

"He doesn't want to see you," Mariah sneered as soon as she saw me.

"That's not for you to decide." I walked briskly past her desk and pushed open his door without knocking. Locking it, I leaned against it as he looked up from a small stack of papers.

Slowly one eyebrow lifted as he watched me.

"Look, we are going to have a talk and I don't need Ms. Thing out there bothering us."

"Let me take care of that." John stood and walked calmly toward me.

If I hadn't seen him the night before, I wouldn't have guessed he was any different than any other day before we'd been together.

"Excuse me. I can't open the door if you insist on leaning on it." He stood only inches away and his delicious scent surrounded me. His eyes were guarded and cold as he looked down at me.

Feeling stupid, I stepped to the side. He opened the door and stuck his head out.

"Leave, now. Lock the office behind you," he demanded with a stern Dom tone of voice before closing it and returning to his perch behind his desk. "Now, what was it you wanted to talk about?"

"How do you know she left?" I glanced at him before looking toward where Mariah was probably listening.

"She will. Would you rather waste time debating on how well my secretary listens to orders or talk about whatever it is that has you in my office so early this morning?" He looked at me expectantly.

"I'd rather avoid all things involving your secretary," I said quietly, but sat in the chair across from him. "I've decided to give you the chance to voice whatever it is that has you still blowing up my phone. Obviously you have something to say."

I couldn't help but be defensive. It wasn't how I'd planned to come to his office and speak with him, but he was so cold, so harsh, I fired back with the same tone, forgetting I was there to help him deal with his pain.

He tilted his head and stared at me for a full minute before nodding as if he had the answer to some unvoiced question.

"I wanted to know if you wanted back the stuff you'd left at my apartment."

I nearly gaped at his response, but I caught myself.

"That's it?" I'd thought he wanted to try to explain himself or try to get me to take him back or something, but he simply wanted to give me my things back?

"Yes. What did you think it was?" He rubbed his thumb over his lower lip, drawing my eyes to them. I felt my heart clench. Not so long ago I would've been free to take those lips any time I wanted; now I could only watch them.

"Nothing." I stood and swallowed. "Well, if you have the time now, we can go get whatever was left behind."

"No. I'll leave you here and retrieve it myself. You are no longer welcome in my place," he said, standing and walking to the door. "Give me five minutes and you can be out of my life forever."

Before I could respond, he was out the front door and I was alone. I took my head in my hands and a sob slipped out unexpectedly. I had to hold it together for a few more minutes. I could do it. Wiping the tears away from my face, I stood and tried to make sure he wouldn't be able to tell how much he was stomping on the shattered pieces of my heart. I realized then that some part of me had harbored the idea that we'd get back together, but this was the end.

The outside door opened and I turned, thinking it would be John, but it was Mariah instead.

"I forgot… Oh, it's just you," Mariah scoffed and strutted closer. Calling out, she said, "John?"

"He stepped out for a minute." I didn't have it in me to say where.

"Oh, well, then it's just you and me. In case you haven't figured it out yet, we're together. We have been for months. John was trying to find a good time to tell you. I actually felt bad for you." Mariah shrugged a delicate shoulder, but her face told me she didn't feel bad at all.

"Really? Interesting that *I* didn't know this." John stood at the door with anger vibrating off him in waves.

"Oh, John!" Mariah spun around to look at him.

"Please, do tell me why you are telling the woman I love that we are fucking when every day I have to fight my repulsion for you." He stepped closer, letting the door swing closed.

"Wait, what?" I looked between them, confused. My head spun as I studdered, "But… all the conversations, the lipstick, the condom."

"Condom?" John briefly glanced at me, but his eyes were burning through Mariah. "You better start talking."

"I was just trying to save you, sir. She isn't good enough for you. Look at her. She's not pretty enough, not submissive enough. You need someone who can give you everything you need. I wanted to get her out of the picture so I could show you how much I've learned since we broke up, how much we are meant to be together." Mariah dropped to her knees and wobbled forward, reaching for his hand.

"What fucking condom?" John barked, stepping out of reach.

Mariah lowered her head, but didn't say anything.

"Answer me!" he shouted.

"I... may have planted a condom in the trash for her to find," Mariah whispered.

"And the lipstick?"

"I brushed my lips against you when I fixed your hair, sir." She shrank into herself.

"But the phone calls..." I interrupted, not understanding why someone would be so cruel.

"No one was on the phone," Mariah answered.

"Get out now. I don't ever want to see you again," John growled as he stepped around her, giving her his back as his attention shifted to me. No longer was he the cold, impersonal man who'd been in his office.

Mariah quietly left and John dropped the box he'd held under his arm, but I hadn't noticed until it banged against the floor. He looked almost scared as he slowly moved closer to me.

"Why didn't you tell me?" he asked, pained.

"I tried. It never came out right and I didn't know who to believe. She was so convincing." I closed my eyes and took a breath. "And I *don't* deserve you. I'm not a good sub. I'm not beautiful."

"Don't." He was pulling me into his arms and sighing. "Don't put yourself down. I love the way you submit to me. I love the way you look. I love you and you are perfect the way you are."

My heart beat again. It came back to life feeling his strength surrounding me, his scent enveloping me, his words pulling all the broken pieces back together.

Chapter 16

John

She was in my arms. I breathed her in. The world righted itself and stopped spinning out of control. I could survive anything as long as I had her in my life. I held her close for a long time. I couldn't seem to make my arms release her.

Finally she shifted and pulled back and I had to let go.

"I missed this," she breathed.

"Me too. God, how I wished you'd talked to me and I hadn't been so stubborn." I cradled her cheek. I hadn't thought I'd ever be free to touch her again. Anger at Mariah raged inside me but was nothing compared to the relief, the feeling that I was once again whole washed over me simply by knowing Alix was mine.

I had been lucky enough to catch the end of their conversation and realization came crashing down upon me that Mariah had been pushing us apart so she could try to get me back. All the times Alix had mentioned she didn't like Mariah and asked questions about her boyfriend suddenly made sense. I just hadn't seen what she was trying to tell me.

"Come on, let's take your things back to my place. In fact, I think you should bring all of your stuff over. Live with me." I watched her carefully as I voiced what I'd wanted to ask her for a long time.

"I don't know. I mean we just went through time apart, John. I think maybe we should take it slow." She forced a smile and I could tell the separation had been as hard on her as it had for me.

"Whatever you want. I'll do anything for you," I whispered, my heart in my throat. I'd said I loved her and she hadn't answered. I wouldn't push for her to return the words, I would wait until she was ready but I wasn't going to let her go ever again.

"Can we take this box back and then go to lunch?" She heaved the box up into her arms and I took it from her.

"Absolutely."

We walked in silence to the hotel and the elevator was filled with tension as we rode up together. It seemed neither one of us wanted to be the first to speak. When I opened the door to my apartment, I couldn't hold back any more.

"Please, come in."

She followed me with a shy smile. I led her toward the bedroom where it would be easiest to unpack the box, since it was mostly clothes and toiletries. Once I set it on the foot of the bed, I turned and was surprised to find Alix right behind me.

"Hi," she rasped as her hands came up to rest on my chest.

"Hi." I automatically wrapped my arms around her, pulling her flush against me.

"Are you okay with this?" She pushed to her toes, her lips almost to mine.

"More than okay."

Leaning down, I closed the remaining distance to seal our mouths together. My body instantly sparked to life in a way it hadn't since she'd left. My cock grew hard simply from the taste of her. The tip of her tongue slid over the seam of my lips before pressing inside.

Alix moaned and leaned into me, her arms clasping my biceps as our tongues slid along each other. Her fingers twisted in my shirt, pulling me into her.

"God, I've missed you," she gasped, breaking the kiss.

Gliding my hands down, I gripped her ass and thrust against her at the same time making sure it was clear how much I agreed with her.

"I want you," she breathed against my lips as our breaths mingled.

"I *need* you."

Her hands yanked on either side of my shirt, ripping apart the buttons so her hands could skim over my chest. A groan rumbled from my chest as she flicked her fingers over my distended nipples. Turning her, I pushed her back onto the bed and yanked the ugly pants from her legs. Skirts looked much better on her sexy body; however, when I realized there was only a tiny pair of panties on under them, I decided they weren't so bad.

I undid my cufflinks, letting them drop before shrugging out of my shirt and toeing off my shoes. Grabbing her hips, I pulled her to the edge of the bed and dropped to my knees. My face was pressed to her pussy before I'd fully hit the ground.

As I flicked my tongue over her swollen bud, she cried out and tightened her thighs around my head while one hand gripped my hair as much as it could. It didn't take much to have her screaming out her release, giving me plenty of her honey to lap up.

While I could eat her all night, my aching cock demanded more. I needed to be in her, feel her pulling me deep and hugging the most sensitive part of my body with hers.

Standing, I roughly slid her panties off before undoing my trousers and letting them fall. With one hand, I guided my cock to her entrance while supporting myself with the other. I wanted to tease her, make it good for her, but my need to reclaim what was mine was too strong to deny any longer.

Just the head of my cock slid into her and I watched as she gasped, fisting the sheets. As I stared down at her, I realized I still hadn't taken off her coat, so I slid the single button through the hole to reveal all she wore underneath

RACHAEL ORMAN

was a bra. My hips surged into her at the surprise of my sexy little vixen.

Pulling on the center of her bra, I forced her to sit up so I could shove the material from her shoulders. Her legs wrapped around me and she leaned back onto one hand while reaching for me with the other. Holding my neck, she yanked me down to meet her lips once more. The bruises and welts on my back screamed out in pain, but I needed her kiss more than anything at that moment.

My hips moved on their own, sinking my cock deep into her as she moved with me. When she broke the kiss, her gaze locked on mine. I could see her arousal, her desire, in her eyes. Even though our lips had parted, she kept a tight grip on the back of my neck, her fingers digging into my flesh.

I grabbed hold of her ponytail and yanked her head back while my other hand dipped between our bodies to tease her clit. She was moaning and panting, but her eyes stayed on mine as I moved hard and fast against her.

My orgasm was gathering at the base of my spine, but I refused to give in. I would not come until she got off at least once more.

Dropping my head, I dragged my teeth over her throat before sucking a chunk and biting down. Alix arched into me as every muscle clenched tightly and she flooded my cock with her release.

She fell onto her back and I gripped her breast harshly as I pounded into her. My nails broke through her skin as my orgasm tore through me and I yelled out. I bathed her insides with my come as my hips slowed and I fought to get my breathing and heart back under control.

"Damn, I really missed that," Alix sighed as she lay limp on the bed. I lowered myself over her and kissed her lips softly.

"Me too, Precious."

"John…" she started, her eyes clouded over. "There is something I want to talk to you about."

I started to pull from her, but she clamped her legs around me, keeping me in her body.

"No, I want you right where you are. It's…" She blew out a breath before meeting my eyes again. "I saw you at the club last night."

My back tensed and I jerked as if she'd slapped me.

"What?" I wheezed the single word painfully.

"I was trying to get over you and thought being with another Dom would help, but instead I got a front-row seat to your scene."

I stared at her, unable to figure out how she felt about what she'd seen, so I went the easier route.

"You scened with another Dom?" It hurt, but I knew we weren't together then so I had no right.

"Yes. His name was Gabe."

"I'm going to kill that motherfucker." I gritted my teeth and yanked back from her, but her legs held tight.

"We didn't have sex. It was just a spanking. I'm glad I did because he showed me what you were going through."

She winced. "That's why I was coming to talk to you today."

"And?" I held my breath, but I understood why she'd been careful not to touch my back. I'd never told her I was bi and worried how she'd feel about it.

"Are you okay? I mean, you were taking quite a beating."

Maybe she hadn't seen everything.

"I'm fine now that I have you back in my life."

She nodded as if she wasn't wholly convinced. "And your desire for men? Were you going to tell me about that?"

She had.

"Alix, there is only one time I am ever with men. When I'm being a submissive, which isn't often," I admitted.

"Do you want to talk about why you were there? Gabe said it had something to do with your past and a trigger of some kind."

I hated discussing such a hard topic when my cock was still in her. I wanted to pace. I wanted to put space between us, but she wasn't allowing it.

"One day I will tell you about it. Not now." I sighed.

"That's what you always say," she said, frowning.

"I can't. We can talk about anything else, but not that. Not today. Please, don't push the topic." I wanted to tell her. I wanted to vent my story, but I couldn't handle any more intense emotions in one day.

"I'm going to keep asking until you tell me," she said finally releasing me. "For now I'll drop it though."

"Thank you," I whispered while closing my eyes.

Withdrawing from her, I used my destroyed shirt to wipe between her legs. The urge to shove my fingers inside her to ensure some of me stayed in her flared through me, but I resisted. Once she was clean, I tossed the shirt aside and pulled my trousers back up. I'd never been so glad I'd skipped underwear, since it gave me one less thing to deal with when I'd been so desperate to fill her.

I held up her panties in one hand and her trousers in the other. She smiled and took them before slipping them on and stepping into the heels I'd knocked off when I'd pulled them from her.

"If you're going without, then I will too." She winked before shrugging her coat back on.

"Does that mean since you're going without a shirt, I should go without one as well?" I fought to not smile. I missed her saucy side and the easy conversations we had. We were back to normal, the tense air gone.

"Mmm. I'd enjoy it, but we don't want to cause a scene. You know, because women won't care that they are married or with their man, they'll drool over all..." She gestured to my chest. "That."

Shaking my head, I laughed and went to my closet for a new shirt. I pulled it on as I returned to her.

"May I?" she asked, holding up my cufflinks in her palm.

"If you wish." I held out one arm for her. I'd never had someone dress me before, but I could get used to it. She slid the small clasp through the buttonholes before clamping it so it was secure. Switching hands, I watched her fingers as she fastened the other one. My cock was already filling from watching her doing something so caring for me.

Once she was done, she tugged my shirt closed and started doing the buttons for me. She glanced up and caught me staring with a stupid smile on my face.

"What?" She frowned.

"Nothing. I like you taking care of me. No one has ever done it before." I shrugged as she did the last button.

"Well, I like taking care of you, so that works out good then." She stepped back and I tucked the shirt into my trousers.

"Ready?" I sat on the bed and pulled on my shoes before tying them.

"Yep."

Placing my hand on her back, I showed her to the elevator. I looked over at her and she smiled at me. How quickly things had gone from the worst day of my life to the best day.

I took her to my favorite restaurant and we talked about how things had been at work. I made sure to avoid anything that had to do with Mariah. Even the thought of her had me gritting my teeth, but I was determined not to let her ruin any time I had with Alix. I would handle her soon enough.

After dinner, I knew I had to do something I'd been putting off, but it was the only way my Dom side would be satisfied after learning she'd seen me as a submissive. I couldn't let her think of me that way. She was my submissive and I was her dominant.

Parking in front of Scene, I turned to her and took her hand.

"Precious, you are to go into our room and prepare yourself for me. Since you don't have panties I expect you to be fully nude and waiting," I told her and watched as arousal filled her eyes along with curiosity. I knew she wanted to take it slow, but I couldn't deny my Dom. He was roaring for me to reassert my control over her. "Do you have a problem with that?"

"No, sir," she didn't hesitate to answer me.

"Go. Now." I released her hand and let her open her own door for the first time. Watching as she crossed the parking lot and disappeared through the doors, I made sure she made it safely inside before following much more sedately. She didn't know it, but I paid her dues for the club. If I was going to be asking her to meet me, then it was my burden to pay for her. I'd started paying before she'd even known who I was and planned to continue to do so.

After giving her more than enough time to strip and kneel, I entered the room. I knew she wasn't a huge fan of kneeling since it tended to hurt her knees, but I'd made sure to give her enough time to anticipate what was coming. In the apartment, we'd been rushed by need. My Dom didn't care for rushing; he was all for dragging things out and taking complete control of her mind and body.

"Stand, Precious, and undress me," I ordered her as I stepped in front of her. She'd followed orders and was on her knees completely nude, thighs spread, palms resting on them. Untying my shoes, she removed them, followed by my socks. She stood and unclamped my cufflinks, bending to put them in one of my shoes before dragging her fingers down my buttons. Yanking my shirt out of my trousers, she started at the bottom and worked her way up unfastening the buttons. Instead of removing my shirt, she dropped her hands to my belt. Once she had it open, she released my pants and followed them down to my ankles to help me step out of them. Standing again, she slid her hands over my skin from my ankles, up my legs and chest to move down my arms. The shirt fell to the ground.

"Excellent," I murmured before grabbing the heavy leather collar from the dresser filled with toys. As I reached to wrap it around her neck, I noticed the absence of her pearls. "No pearls?"

"N...no, sir." She bowed her head in shame. "I took them off when I thought you no longer wanted me."

"I will always want you," I stated emphatically. "You will wear this collar until I can place your pearls back on you."

Her head snapped up in surprise. The collar wasn't something anyone would mistake for anything other than what it was. It was a punishment in itself, but I hated her not wearing something to signify my ownership of her. I did own her, too. She was mine forever, no matter what else happened.

"Yes, sir," she said after a moment.

I clipped a chain to the metal loop in the front of the collar, then turned toward the door.

"You will be getting that punishment I promised you so long ago," I told her before walking out the door. I felt a slight hesitation from her before she followed quietly behind me. Once we entered the main room, I led her to the back of the large empty room with a solitary wooden bench that was larger than the spanking benches. I heard a soft gasp from her, but didn't slow my pace.

As I turned to face her, I saw Gabe walk in and smiled wickedly.

"Anyone who wishes to watch is more than welcome," I said to him. He nodded and I turned my attention to Alix. "Say stop and this ends."

"I remember, sir," she swallowed.

"Then lie down, beautiful." I stepped back, letting her leash drop as I grabbed the machine from the corner of the room. Turning around, I couldn't help but gaze at my lovely woman as she sprawled over the bench. Her arms were already over her head, ready to be restrained, while her legs were spread so her feet touched the floor. I walked closer, taking the machine with me, and I felt my cock elongate when my eyes landed on her bare pussy. It was already glistening with her eagerness and I yearned to taste it.

No, not until after her punishment, the Dom in my head barked.

Pushing the machine to the foot of the bench, I maneuvered the vibrating tip to her clit while lining up the automatic thrusting cock to her opening. I used two fingers to enter her and she moaned, arching her back.

Yes, she was ready for her punishment. Wet and willing.

"There is a dial here for me to control the vibrations and the speed at which you will be fucked," I informed her as I turned it on. I watched as the realistic looking cock slowly slid into her and she cried out. "Feel good?"

"Not as good as you, sir," she moaned and I turned the dial up, adding in the vibrator. She writhed, reminding me I hadn't yet secured her. I was getting ahead of myself since I was so excited to watch her being fucked without my own orgasm getting in the way.

I used the leather cuffs attached to the bench to tie down her ankles to the legs of the bench before using the cuffs at the top to restrain her wrists. Returning to the machine, I watched as it filled her, then receded.

There were voices growing in strength and I looked up to find we had been joined by a crowd. Some were watching while others were being sucked or fucked. I reached down to take my dick in my hand and found there was a copious amount of pre-come leaking from my tip.

Using the moisture, I pumped my fist over my cock a few times while watching Alix. I moved my hand lazily up and down since there was no rush to come.

Alix cried out her first orgasm and I smiled. As I knelt next to her head, she turned to look at me.

"Who is your master?" I demanded.

"You are, sir." She bit down on her bottom lip.

"Who owns your body?"

"You do, sir."

"Who owns your pleasure?"

"You, sir."

"That's right, now show me how beautiful you are when you come. I want this table covered with your come when we are done. You are mine and I want every person in this building to hear you crying out with the pleasure I give you — even when it becomes too much and it hurts, I want you to come again and again. No one else is ever to give you pleasure. It is all mine. Mine to control, mine to give." I fondled her breasts as I spoke to her, causing her to moan and move with the machine.

"Yes, master. I am your's." She paused to suck in a breath. "My body is yours to do with as you please."

"That's right. Don't ever forget it."

She cried out and came again, her gaze on mine as she did.

"Never, sir," she breathed.

I stepped back and spotted a riding crop under the table. Smiling, I picked it up and ran the tip around her nipples.

"Mmm, look what I found, Precious." I traced her jaw with it. She groaned with pleasure as she closed her eyes. I waited until I could tell she was on the brink of coming again and then brought the crop down on one nipple, then the other. She exploded and yelled out louder than before with her release.

I used the crop all over her breasts and even parts of her stomach as she was forced to come again and again. Deciding she'd had enough of the additional pain, I dropped the crop back to where I'd found it. She was moaning in pain from the number of forced orgasm, but still she didn't say to stop. While she could keep taking it, I couldn't.

Standing next to her, I clutched at my cock. I jerked my hand up and down my length roughly until finally thick strands shot from my tip, all over her stomach. She got off at the same time, obviously enjoying the added benefit of watching me play with my dick.

I placed a palm over my release and rubbed it into her skin.

"Mine," I growled as I kept rubbing until it had dried, leaving a crusty residue behind. My cock was still hard though, so I moved to kneel over her chest. "Suck."

She lifted her head and even though she was breathing hard, she took me into her mouth. Holding the back of her head, I supported her as she moved rapidly up and down. At one point, she paused to moan around me as she came yet again. As soon as she came down, she started sucking again.

Adding her teeth into the mix, she had me thrusting into her, forcing her to take me deeper. Sparks started to gather in my balls and I clenched at her hair, which was still in the horrible ponytail. My thighs trembled. My eyes closed. When I couldn't take anymore, I yelled, "Come. Now."

She bucked against me as much as her restraints allowed and I filled her throat with my seed. I nearly collapsed on top of her from coming so hard, but managed not to, barely. After a second, I climbed off her and turned the machine off.

"Good girl, Precious," I said, pushing it out of the way. Undoing her restraints, I helped her sit up. Her eyes were glossed over as she looked at me. My sweet girl was well into subspace. Gathering her to my chest, I glanced around to see everyone was in various stages of fucking. The ones who didn't do public scenes must've left or given into their desires. I couldn't blame them. Watching her had been too much for me to handle without needing to get my own release as well.

Gabe appeared at my side and I stared at him while soothing a hand over Alix's back.

"I see things are going well between you two," he said, nodding toward her.

"Seems that way." I was still pissed he'd interfered in my life, but then if he hadn't I quite possibly wouldn't have Alix back.

"It's good to see you back acting as a Dom. You thrive as a Dom."

"I thrive because she is at my side, nothing else." I placed a kiss on the top of her head. "I love her. She is my world and I was stupid to not fight harder, to let my demons get the better of me."

"We all have our own demons and handle them our own way. You know I'm here for you and would do anything to help a good friend out. I'm glad she followed my advice and your stubborn ass listened." Gabe smiled before walking away.

I couldn't help but smile too.

Chapter 17

Alix

When I floated back to my body, I found John and I were in his room at the club, cuddled together.

"Welcome back," he said as his hand continued to run over my head, comforting me.

My lady parts were sore for the first time in a very, very long time. Where John's nails had broken the skin of my breasts stung, especially after he'd taken the crop to them, but it had felt amazing when he'd done it. Every part of me was content, my mind at ease after such an intense scene and being back where I belonged -- in John's arms.

"Mmm." I snuggled more deeply into his chest, reveling in his hard muscles.

"Yes, I do believe that's exactly how I feel," John laughed softly. "How are *you* feeling, Precious?"

"Good, but sore," I croaked, my throat dry.

"Was it too much?"

"No. It was perfect."

I felt him relax under me as if some unknown tension I hadn't realized was there had dissipated.

"You are perfect." He gently tugged on my hair until I was looking up at him. My ponytail was no more. He must have removed it at some point. "You are, you know."

"Hardly," I scoffed, but smiled. He was the perfect one. Maybe not to everyone else, but to me he was exactly what I needed, wanted. Staring up at him, I realized I wanted to give him everything. I wanted to stay with him forever. I wanted to live with him. When he'd first asked, I'd hesitated, worried something from his past would come up again and I wouldn't be able to handle it. Separating from him while having no where to live would've only made it so much worse, but I realized we'd have to work our problems out if we lived together. "I'm going to need your help."

"Anything."

"Well, you see, this incredibly wonderful man asked me to move in with him, but I have a lot of stuff. I have a house I'll need to rent or sell. There are a lot of things I need assistance with if I want to make it happen." I watched as light blossomed in his eyes as it what I was saying sank in.

"You'll move in?" he asked, shocked. It had only been hours since I'd refused his offer. "What changed?"

"You reminded me of everything we have together. How much I need you from the time I wake up to the time I fall asleep with your arms wrapped tightly around me. I can't go back to sleeping alone. I don't want to. I want to smell your morning breath and hear you snoring in the middle of the night. All of it. You being there when I get home from an exhausting day at work or when I need someone to vent to about horrible clients. Just you, all the time." I planted a kiss on his slightly parted lips. "Do you still want me?"

"Absolutely," he breathed against my mouth before closing the distance for a passion-fueled kiss. "Nothing would make me happier."

"I do have a confession to make though."

"Really? And what might that be?" He lifted his eyebrow.

"When we were apart… I broke rules," I sighed. I really wasn't up for another punishment, not so soon after the one I'd just gone through, but I wanted him to know everything.

"Hmm." He pursed his lips. "Broke the rules, hmm?"

"Yes, sir. I masturbated many times a day. The compulsions were back stronger than ever before," I admitted. I shifted away from him, feeling the crusty layer on my stomach. A shower was in order as soon as we made it through this conversation.

"Do you feel the compulsion now?" he asked, tilting his head.

"No, sir. I know that you will provide all the pleasure I need." It was the truth — somehow when he was around, I no longer felt the need to touch myself or fulfill the compulsions I knew I'd probably always feel. Addictions never fully went away, as I had learned; it was simply having the tools to handle it that made me not give in. John was the best thing for me.

"Then I suppose I can let it slide. We were both in dark places and doing things that weren't good for us." I could tell from the glint in his eye he was remembering how he'd coped. I knew I'd never forget what I saw. The marks on his back would take a long time to fully heal so I'd have reminders of it until then. He barely seemed to notice them, which told me he'd been whipped more than once and was used to the residual pain from them. Thankfully, although he'd been whipped numerous times, the skin hadn't been broken a single time.

I couldn't help but wonder what he'd been through — what else was this man hiding about his past? While I didn't want to push, I knew soon enough I would be poking around for answers. The only way we would ever last is if we finally shared all our demons. I would have to put mine out there as well and I wasn't ready to do it yet, so I let him keep his secrets for a while longer.

Epilogue

John

Since I was without a secretary, I didn't want to have to work, but I also had a lot of appointments to reschedule from taking the day off unexpectedly to fuck Alix senseless. That night while we lay in bed, she played on her phone while I glanced through résumés.

We had to figure out what to do with her house and get her moved in, but knowing she wanted to live with me was enough for now. The rest could come later.

She slapped her hand on the mattress and turned toward me with a huge smile on her face. "That's it! I know who will be your secretary!" she exclaimed excitedly.

"Who?" She hadn't mentioned anything about it before then so I really had no idea who she was talking about.

"Jennifer! She works downstairs and I think she'd be perfect. She's a freak and super energetic. We were just talking and she said something about being tired of her job. I bet she'd fit in perfectly at your practice." I'd never seen Alix so eager and excited about something outside of the bedroom or playroom.

"I don't know," I sighed, scratching my cheek while thinking about the perky woman I'd met many times. "She's a little *too* energetic. I would have to deal with her every day and that might drive me crazy."

"Oh, baby, I would help calm you down whenever you needed some release," she soothed, running a hand over my bare chest.

"Let me think about it."

"Okay." She pouted and sat back defeatedly.

The next day I found myself welcoming Jennifer into the office so I could show her around. Turned out Alix was pretty good at convincing me to see things her way when she really wanted to. I couldn't complain too much, as getting a replacement for Mariah so quickly would save me quite a few headaches. It didn't matter to me she hadn't given a two-week notice. The hotel would easily be able to replace her while it was much harder to get someone competent to work for me.

Before I knew it, the day was over. Between training Jennifer and calling my appointments to reschedule, the hours had flown by. Not to mention Alix stopped by at lunch time for a quickie on my desk. Yet again it turned out she made me forget where I was and what I normally did when she put her mind to it.

As I walked out of the building to collect Alix from the hotel, I spotted a blonde I would happily never see again. Mariah.

"This isn't over, John. You are mine and I am not giving up on you so easily," she said before walking away from me.

I had a stalker of my own it appeared. One who was hell-bent on destroying my relationship with Alix.

No, things with Mariah weren't over. I would have to warn Alix and figure out a way to make Mariah see we were over no matter what she thought.

To Be Continued…

More Books By Rachael Orman

In The Moment
Part One - *FREE*
Part Two
Part Three
Part Four – Coming April 13
Part Five – Coming April 27

Her Series
Her Ride (Ryan & Ellis)
Her Journey (Melia & Patrick)
Her Run (Blaze & Monk) – Coming May 2015

Cravings Series
Lost Desires - *FREE*
Addict - *FREE*
Fiend

Yearning Series (M/F/F Menage)
Yearning Devotion
Yearning Absolution

Other Works
In Flight (M/F/M Menage – Short Story)
Loneliness Ebbs Deep – CoWritten by Adrian J. Smith – F/F –
Monster Erotica
Love is a Mess Anthology – Bar Tryst (F/F Short)

Made in United States
North Haven, CT
24 June 2024